INFILTRATION

BOOK ONE OF MURPHY'S LAWLESS: MISSION CRITICAL

Griffin Barber

Beyond Terra Press
Coinjock, NC

Chris Kennedy/Beyond Terra Press
1097 Waterlily Rd.
Coinjock, NC 27923
https://chriskennedypublishing.com/

Cover Art and Design by Thomas Peters.

Edited by Charles E. Gannon.

Ordering Information:
Quantity sales. Special discounts are available on quantity purchases by corporations, associations, and others. For details, contact the "Special Sales Department" at the address above.

Infiltration/Griffin Barber -- 1st ed.
ISBN: 978-1648552274

This book is dedicated to the people who helped me become a better person.

Backsliding

Chalmers wilted as he stepped into the light of both suns. The temperature rose by twenty degrees in that single step. At least the cold worry-sweat he'd built up waiting in the hospital ward wouldn't be so out of place.

Much of the base was being pulled down around them. Word had just arrived from the secret SpinDog colony—*Spin One*—that the next wave of ships from Kulsis was approaching the planetary system; the Lost Soldiers were being pulled out and any overt evidence of their presence—like the base—was being hastily wiped from the face of R'Bak.

"Why are you *such* a dick, Chalmers?" Jackson asked, shoving the door open and walking up the shallow, rammed-earth ramp to join his partner. Most buildings on R'Bak used the earth to help keep them cool, and the field hospital was no exception, despite its temporary nature.

"Am I?" Chalmers asked, hating the defensive tone that crept into his voice. He started walking toward *Man-Eater*. They had orders to meet up with the Big Cheese before they bugged out. He wasn't sure what the meeting was for. It wasn't like they'd have time for a mission before the Kulsis surveyors were close enough to see what was going on in orbit, let alone on the ground.

Jackson caught up with Chalmers, hitting him in the chest with the back of one hand. "I thought you were done with this kind of shit, man."

"Look, it's not my fault Murphy is dragging us away from your new bestie while he's laid up in hospital."

Jackson stopped walking and rounded on his partner. Chalmers expected his expression to be angry, but Jackson's face was suspicious. Not an angry, "you screwed me again" suspicious, but the, "I know what's going on now," kind of suspicion that was generally a lot worse.

"That's what this shit is about, isn't it?" Jackson's voice had gone up an octave, another bad sign. "Why you were such a relentless dick on the radio every time El called in."

Chalmers didn't slow down. He didn't want to have this conversation. Not now, not ever.

Jackson followed after him, grabbed his shoulder, and forced Chalmers to look him in the face. "I was wondering why you were being such a relentless dick to El, and I just figured it out. You're jealous. You're fucking *jealous.*"

Chalmers raised his hands without quite knowing what to do with them. Wanting to say something witty, he came up short, and said, "Bullshit." The lie lacked conviction, even to his own ears.

"No, I think I'm on the money. It hurts your poor little ego that I'm buddies with El, and so you took it out on him."

Chalmers, as he had so often in his misspent life, scoffed at the truth. The truth hurt, so ignore it. The truth could wound, so dodge that shit like a bullet.

"You have friends. I only have you," he wanted to say, but couldn't. He'd promised to be the better man, but some situations made it a lot harder to live up to that promise than others.

"Look, man," he said aloud, "we got places to be." He turned and quick-marched the last few strides to the buggy.

Jackson muttered a string of expletives Chalmers could barely hear but followed after him. He was still shaking his head in disbelief as he climbed into the passenger seat.

Dropping into the battered vehicle, Chalmers kicked *Man-Eater's* powerful engine over and put her in gear.

*****

Briefing

Murphy kicked the briefing room door closed behind his Russian adjutant. If he resented the interruption from his subordinate, it didn't show as he returned to the head of the long table that dominated the room.

"This operation will also be entirely clandestine: no uniforms, no copies of familiar weapons, and very little logistics other than what our groundside allies can furnish, though I have sureties from them that they will furnish everything necessary to ease your way into the local market. Comms will also be slow as well as intermittent, as we will not be able to risk transmitting in the vicinity of the island. In short, Operation Wormwood is a go, gentlemen," Murphy said, bringing the informational portion of the briefing to an end. "Questions, comments, concerns?"

"Shit," Chalmers whispered, letting his chair fall to all four legs. "Where to begin?"

"A question," Murphy leveled that cold stare at him, "Chief?"

"More a number of concerns, sir. We've barely heard of this couple, this Umaren and Vizzel, and you want us to turn them?"

"Two things. One: they already feel obligated to Sergeant Frazier for his aid. Two: I'd have thought they were your kind of people."

"*My* kind of people?" Chalmers asked, incredulous.

Beside him, Jackson covered a grin with one hand. He always seemed to enjoy it when Murphy—or any authority, for that matter—called "bullshit" on Chalmers' behavior.

Murphy raised his hands. "Smugglers, Chalmers. Not…not the other thing."

Chalmers didn't know whether to be more offended or less. He did know that if they'd been back on Earth, in the regular Army, and he'd not made a personal promise to be better, he might have considered threatening a complaint against Murphy under Don't Ask, Don't Tell. But none of those situations applied, so he said simply, "Left all that behind in the Mog, sir. Turned over a new leaf, sir."

Beside him, Jackson's arms wrapped around his chest as if he was struggling to prevent a cough. Chalmers knew it for an attempt to stifle a chuckle. Every NCO worth his salt knew how 'sir' rhymed with 'cur,' and when and where that mental translation should be applied. This being one such instance.

Murphy, never having been an NCO, missed it. In fact, his cold stare thawed slightly as it hung a moment on the fresh shrapnel scars on Chalmers' face. "Indeed you have. I simply want you to employ your considerable…powers for good, this time."

"Understood, sir," Chalmers said more easily. But because he couldn't entirely let it go, he added, "Not for nothing, but I'll have you know my people were bootleggers, Colonel."

"And that's different, how?" Murphy's eyes tightened with that cold look that made Chalmers nervous.

"For one, we wasn't crossing no borders, sir, just county lines." Chalmers continued in his thickest southern drawl, "For 'nother, my people never ran drugs nor evah carried guns. Just relied on speed an' knowin' t'back roads better'n t'revenuers."

Murphy cocked an eyebrow, the very set of his jaw radiating disbelief.

"My *people* never did," Chalmers repeated in a more understandable accent. "What *I* did in the Mog...and...elsewhere was not what my people were into."

His partner shifted uncomfortably in his seat. Chalmers avoided looking at him. They never talked openly about some of the more shady shit he'd been up to his neck in, not really. It wasn't necessary, not in the new universe they found themselves in, not after the things they'd been through together here.

Murphy shook his head. "While I enjoy hearing family histories as much as the next man, the need for your old skills—however acquired—persists. The nature of the ongoing threat the next wave of Kulsian ships poses to R'Bak dictates that we gather as much intelligence as quickly as we can on the island, its personnel, its security, and any and all vulnerabilities of the same."

"So you want someone to buddy up with the seaplane crew, set up a smuggling ring?" Jackson said.

Murphy nodded, shrugged. "From the report, the crew is already embedded in the black market, so it will be more, 'making use of' than 'setting up.' I leave exactly how you do up to you. I think that is the best route available, but I'll rely on your combined expertise."

"If I may, sir, I have additional concerns."

Murphy nodded permission.

"Will we will be the only Lost Soldiers on R'Bak?"

"Eventually, and for a time, yes. We will continue pulling our conventional formations and cadre out to keep the incoming surveyors from learning the extent to which the R'Baku have had outside aid. We need the Kulsis survey guys fat and happy, or at least ignorant, so they don't go running back to Kulsis for forces sufficient to hunt the SpinDogs down."

"Leaving aside questions of just how much of our presence here can be concealed, sir, I don't see how much a couple of investigators can reasonably expect to accomplish."

"As I informed you in the briefing, expectations are not excessive, Chief," Murphy said. "We know your capabilities, and the SpinDogs are confident that the surveyors are, for the most part, unexceptional and incurious. People without much in the way of prospects on Kulsis who are here to collect the wealth of their superiors and return home with it."

Chalmers shook his head, deciding that particular subject was a dead issue. "What other assets will we have? The briefing was slim on details."

"In time, I'll be sending a couple of other specialists. Messina, first, I think."

"Who?" Chalmers and Jackson asked.

"A Vietnam-era security specialist. Due to recent events, we need him moved off the habitats, making him free to pull security for you and the crew."

And watchdog us, Chalmers thought.

"Very good, sir. Thank you, sir," Jackson said. "But I think the Chief meant assets in terms of high value items we can use to purchase cooperation from the indigs and, eventually, the Kulsians?"

"Ah, right. I'll arrange for our groundside allies to provide a selection of drugs, both recreational and medical, to trade with. We should also be able to arrange more specialized goods, given enough lead time and good reason."

"Makes sense, sir," Jackson said. Glancing at Chalmers to make sure he wasn't interrupting, he went on, "One question, sir: when can we expect Elroy to get healthy? I'd asked the healers but they weren't very forthcoming. I only ask because El—Sergeant Frazier—would be a big help in turning the crew our way." Chalmers could hear the concern for the other man in Jackson's voice.

A pained look flashed across the colonel's face before disappearing behind the cold mask of his habitual calm. "That is unknown. Sergeant Frazier did himself considerable damage. The healers have not been optimistic about his return to full duty."

"Damn, sir," Chalmers said, glancing at Jackson. "I didn't think it was that serious."

"Does he know?" Jackson asked after a moment spent waiting for the colonel to continue.

"Know what?" Murphy asked.

"Does he know he might not make it back to Mar—Major Lee's crew?"

"I will make the appropriate notifications as and when necessary, Sergeant Jackson." He relented slightly, adding, "I'm told he needs to focus on getting better just now."

Jackson opened his mouth to say something Chalmers knew he'd regret, so he spoke first, "The Clarthu are big on a good attitude leading to faster healing. A lot more than our docs were, back in the day."

"The SpinDog doctors do think in those terms," Murphy agreed, a strange expression Chalmers didn't recognize escaping his control for an instant.

Jackson gave a slow nod Chalmers chose to interpret as thanks for stepping in. He was still angry, though, so Chalmers changed the subject. "I assume we'll be using the plane trips to make our reports and pick up any contraband we'll be bringing in, Colonel?"

"Yes. We should be able to arrange a dead drop and commo bunker easily enough. And, when the time comes, we'll use the seaplane to connect other assets into your network as well."

"I bring it up, sir, because the indig crew is a critical failure point, and we don't know to what extent, if any, they'll buy in."

Colonel Murphy nodded. "Correct on all points, Chief. That's where we'll be forced to rely on their expressed debt of gratitude to Sergeant Frazier for saving the young crewman's life. We also plan to make them very wealthy and will rely on your ability to persuade both of them it is in their best self-interest."

"Didn't think you had this much faith in my ability as a salesman, Colonel."

A cold smile. "With Jackson's help, I'm sure you'll manage."

"And we'll be deployed on this op for a while, then?"

"Correct. You will be. Rest assured that I have someone in mind for ongoing intelligence operations once you've established a beachhead. Certain other dominoes have to fall before we can begin that phase, however."

Chalmers nodded, pulling his lip thoughtfully. "So, to summarize: we'll need to introduce ourselves, first, and that'll be harder to do without Sergeant Frazier, but we'll manage. Once we get a feel for where that relationship can take us, we start working our way up the food chain and into the more secure areas of the island. When we have a good idea of the lay of the land, we'll know better what we can accomplish. Is that correct?"

"Yes, Chief."

"Good. Then, I'd like some arms in addition to the drugs. Good to have on hand for bribes or other work, as needed?" He looked a question at Murphy.

"You'll have them."

"Good to know." He glanced again at Jackson, wondering if his only friend was still angry with him for treating El like shit. Taking a deep breath, he addressed Murphy again, "We'll be on our own, for a couple months, right?"

"At least two months, as many as six or more." From Murphy's expression, it was clear he didn't want to go back over ground already trodden. "Consider it a vacation from military discipline and any requirement of wearing a uniform."

Chalmers shook his head. He was looking for an answer to a question he wasn't all that clear on himself. "This will be a long deployment without backup or extraction, on a mission we were never formally trained to do. It's not exactly what we—" he was about to say, 'signed up for,' but settled on, "—are used to."

Murphy's gaze wasn't—quite—as cold as it could get, but dropped to within a few degrees of its minimum possible temperature. "Just now joining the club, are we?"

Chalmers raised his hands in surrender. "Colonel, I'm not saying the rest of the Lost Soldiers ain't been handling rough business...God knows they have!" He looked at Jacks and rushed ahead, "But Sergeant Jackson here doesn't have to get saddled with another risky detail because I've got limited utility and a shitty record."

Jackson's surprised glance at Chalmers was missed by neither its subject nor Murphy.

Murphy's cold gaze warmed a few degrees. "Chief, Sergeant Jackson has made no request for reassignment."

Jackson nodded sharply.

"Until and *if*, he should make such a request, I am not about to break up a proven team that I can rely on to adapt and fill the odd hole in my roster for those missions that require a high degree of adaptation to circumstances and spur-of-the-moment improvisation. This mission will not only rely a great deal on your extra-curricular experience, but also draw on your investigative experience."

Chalmers swallowed a lump in his throat, surprised at how much even an oblique compliment from Colonel Murphy meant to him. Or maybe it was the confirmation that Jackson wasn't trying to get away from him. To cover for the sudden weird surge of pride, he asked, "When do you want to see results, sir?"

"Our best guess is a couple months or so to get the initial groundwork laid, make introductions, etc.," Murphy said. "Then we start phase two."

"Phase two?"

Murphy nodded. "Additional assets in place, we start making moves. You'll understand if I do not go into specifics just now."

Jackson and Chalmers both nodded.

"That said," Murphy continued, "subsequent actions through the network may be on a much tighter timescale, given strategic considerations and the needs of the moment."

"Understood, sir," Chalmers said, looking at his partner for confirmation.

Jackson nodded.

*****

Selling It

"Hey there, Umaren," Chalmers said with a wave.

Umaren turned on his heel and stalked away, grumbling.

"Wait," Chalmers said, striding after the seaplane captain. He quickly caught up with the shorter indig. "What did I say?"

"Maybe show some respect," Jackson offered, *sotto voce.* He continued more loudly, and with better, more polite R'Bakuun than Chalmers could summon, "Umaren, please wait. I apologize for my partner's flippant greeting. It was not proper, but I assure you we have nothing but respect for you, your crew, and your fine seaplane."

The man slowed, stopped. Not wishing to crowd him, Jackson and Chalmers stopped a few paces behind him as well.

"El wanted to thank you for getting him home," Jackson added.

Umaren turned, squinted at Jackson, then up at the taller Chalmers. His brown eyes softened. "He is well?"

"Not entirely. Yet he is far better than he would be had you not brought him into our care." You couldn't lie to an asset you were going to have to rely on for your own skin. Not if you wanted to create the necessary bonds of trust. You could avoid, downplay, even mislead, but outright and easily-refutable lies were best avoided. "He told me to tell you that you and Vizzel were free of any debt to him."

Chalmers cast a worried glance at Jackson. There was telling the truth and then there was being unnecessarily open about the state of play.

Umaren looked down and scuffed the rocky beach with his boot. "The debt is not paid in full. Vizzel is fully recovered and both our lives were saved by El's quick action. I owe him service."

Chalmers had always admired his partner's ability to get a target talking, but this was entirely next level.

"*We* owe him service," another man said, emerging from behind a stretch of rocky shore not five paces from them with a compact and lethal-looking pump shotgun in hand. It wasn't aimed at either Jackson or Chalmers, but it was in hand, and the implicit threat wasn't lost on either Lost Soldier.

Chalmers flinched, showing his shitty startle response once again. He kept his hand from going for his pistol, but only barely.

"Greetings. Vizzel, I take it?" Jackson said, shifting gears without dropping a beat. Chalmers noted his hands hadn't even twitched.

Umaren looked at Vizzel and sighed. "You were to remain hidden."

"And you were to listen to their offer, not walk away like a sullen boy at the first opportunity," the younger man said.

Umaren's hands balled into fists, but he gritted his teeth and returned his attention to the Lost Soldiers.

Jackson smiled at both men. "Why don't we have a drink or two and discuss what might be?"

"What might be?" Umaren and Vizzel chorused with equally puzzled expressions.

"Indeed, what might be a very bright future for you and yours," Jackson said.

"There is only *us*, the crew of *Loklis.* No house, family, or clan; only us and the contract we have with our investors," Umaren said. "El might not have told you this."

Jackson's smile was broad and very, very white in the bright sunshine. "And if I were to tell you that's exactly what I meant?"

Both men looked puzzled.

"For one, we do not hold your relationship as other than normal. With us you could live openly, freely, *richly*."

"I just want to fly," Umaren said. At least partially true, too. Chalmers didn't miss the desperate glance the older man cast at his lover, though.

Vizzel was less cautious than the older man, however. "What do you want from us?"

Jackson cocked his head. "First, let's get off the beach and have a few drinks. Get to know one another a little, then we can try and figure out what we can do for one another."

Chalmers sent yet another grateful prayer to the long-dead and nameless Army personnel clerk who'd condemned Jackson to working with him all those years ago.

Jackson shot a look at his partner that said, *I sold it, you close it.*

* * * * *

Buying It

"He'll kill us rather than release us from our contract," Umaren said, brown eyes wide.

Chalmers followed the pilot's gaze. Umaren's primary investor was easily recognizable, if not by the haughty expression on his face, then by the stylized bird painted on his forehead as well as the bodyguard of, at a quick count, six thugs that surrounded him. He and his entourage had crossed the square, those few patrons of the cafés and bars not too intoxicated to know better quickly getting out of the way.

They'd set up the meet in public in hopes that Umaren's investor, Maktim, would be less inclined to violence with witnesses at hand. In retrospect, that might have been a mistake. From the look on Maktim's face, a public airing of this dispute might just drive him to greater violence.

"Hasn't killed anyone, yet," Chalmers said, hand unconsciously checking the holstered sidearm riding his hip under his light night robes.

"And won't if we have anything to say about it," Jackson added. Chalmers saw his partner already had his gun out under the table. Chalmers swallowed. Jackson ready for trouble was both good and bad: that he always knew *when* shit was about to pop off was good. That didn't mean Chalmers *liked* it when shit was popping off.

Maktim, owner-proprietor of Whikmari Global Transport—an appropriate name for a two-seaplane-and-a-couple-dozen-trucks-operation—strode forward with a sneer on his painted lips. To be fair, he was a very big deal in these parts. For a private, non-Kulsian enterprise to keep and maintain so much technology on R'Bak when the overlords were not present was exceedingly rare. Chalmers had been worried about displacing him, but Umaren had told them that hostile takeover attempts were not uncommon and would raise few alarms.

Chalmers stood, offered a half-bow. "Wel—"

The man ignored him, slammed a hand down on their table. Fruit-and-drink-laden crockery shivered and bounced. "Get your ass to my office, Umaren."

"I-I—" Umaren stammered.

"Umaren is no longer in your employ, Maktim," Chalmers said, surprised at how reasonable his own voice sounded.

The man's eyes slid to Chalmers. "And who are you to speak to me?"

"One of his new partners," Chalmers said, gesturing with his off hand at Umaren. He added a friendly smile. The smile died as he realized the man's pupils were pinpricks despite the dim lantern light of the square.

Shit. Maktim was high as fuck.

"We have a contract." A finger jabbed at Umaren and the thumb of the same hand cocked back at his own chest. "You are not party to that contract."

"A fact we recognize. You will be compensated for his departure from your service."

"I am not selling my interest." Maktim sneered at Chalmers. "So you can crawl back to whatever whore spawned you and beg forgiveness for your failings."

Chalmers glanced past the would-be shipping magnate. His thugs were tense: white knuckles on belts, sweat streaking paint, dry lips licked by dry tongues.

Shit. This was just like the old days in Mog, with the local militia chewing *khat* until they were wound tight as a drum and had to let go. He glanced at Jackson. His partner's face wore that almost-bored expression that told Chalmers he was ready for anything.

"Be reasonable, Maktim," Chalmers said, keeping his voice level and cool to avoid triggering anyone. "Things don't have to be this w—" Chalmers yelped as Jackson kicked him, hard, in the thigh. He lurched sideways just as a forearm-length blade whispered through the space where he'd been.

Chalmers felt his nuts draw up even as Jackson's hand appeared with his gun leveled. The local-made pistol barked twice, pushing needles into Chalmers' ears. The swordsman—Chalmers refused to call any weapon that long a knife—fell on that side of the table, the back of his skull made a mess by a ten-millimeter bullet. His weight half-flipped the table, as well. Crockery shattered on the pavers.

Umaren helped the table along, heaving their end up and over to provide some cover.

Chalmers stood gaping beside it, catching events in flashes: screams and shouts of alarm from bystanders, a general scramble as they fled or dove for cover, Maktim's angry painted face disappearing beyond the table.

One of the thugs standing to the side raised a big revolver and started to cock the hammer. Jackson turned and, without really seeming to aim, cracked off another pair of shots. The thug grunted, wheezed, and collapsed on his ass, pistol clattering on the pavers.

Finally diving behind the table, Chalmers struggled to pull his own pistol. He skidded on some fallen fruit but sat up behind the dubious cover of the cafe table. His hands were clumsy, refusing to pull the pistol free.

Jackson shot several more times.

Chalmers *still* couldn't get his pistol free.

"Red!" Jackson shouted. A faint clatter heard as his spent mag clattered on the pavement. A part of Chalmers was amazed he could hear anything after the gunfire.

An axe bit into the wood next to Chalmers' head.

A fucking *axe!*

A man's head appeared behind the weapon and pulled it free in a shower of splinters. The thug started to step over the table.

"Up!" Jackson shouted.

Hoping his partner could drill the man, Chalmers glanced that way but Jackson was already shooting at someone opposite his side of the impromptu barrier.

Chalmers threw himself backward, pistol finally coming free of the holster inside his robes. He fired from the hip. Bullets tore through light fabric, air, fabric once more, and found flesh and finally, bone, at the far end.

The axe-man stumbled but kept coming across the table at him.

Umaren appeared and threw himself against the thug, his arm traveling from his belt line up under his opponent's rib cage. His knife-hand came away red. He repeated the motion three, four, five times in quick succession.

Shot at least once, stabbed multiple times, the dying man still dragged the pilot to the ground. Not wanting to hit Umaren, Chalmers got in close, pushing his muzzle, robes and all, against the man's skull. He pulled the trigger. The man stilled, the deformed bullet that killed him ricocheting off wet pavers and away with an evil whine.

Scrambling upright, Chalmers risked a look over the table.

Maktim was crawling away, a thick trail of blood glistening in the torchlight from the table to his belly. Another of the thugs was wailing while clutching a hand that appeared to be short a few fingers. The last two thugs had thought better of the fight and were hastily fleeing for the far end of the square.

A furious Chalmers finally extricated his pistol from his tattered, bloody robes.

"Decide to join the fight, did you?" Jackson said, eyes flicking to the gun in Chalmers' hand.

Chalmers shivered. "Couldn't let you have all the glory, could I?"

Jackson's smile was just the slightest bit crazy as he waved at the dead and wounded. "I don't think Maktim will have any more objections to Umaren breaking his contract, do you?"

"Probably not," Chalmers said, feeling a twinge of concern for his friend. Jacks was better than Chalmers at mayhem. Didn't make the sergeant easy with it. Not normally. "You all right?"

"Right enough. Street rules rule here, just like the South Side."

Chalmers let that ride and said: "You hurt?"

"No, you?"

"Nope. Umaren?"

The pilot spread his arms wide. "None of this is mine."

"Good. Looks like you're a free agent now."

Umaren walked over and spat on the now-still form of his former boss. "Good."

*****

Customs

Chalmers looked around, too keyed up to enjoy the play of cool air on his painted skin while they waited to be seen by the customs official. The terminal building of the airport was half-underground but had all the modern conveniences—like air conditioning—Chalmers hadn't seen anywhere but SpinDog habs since waking up. The facility also had a number of security and civilian officials in a variety of uniforms and face paint. At least the camera mounts for the surveillance system sat empty on the walls. The reavers were, according to Umaren, tasked with getting such tech up and running. But the destruction of all their spaceside assets and the wide scattering of those on the planet had rendered such tasks not only impossible, but pointless.

Umaren had said the customs official they were required to meet with would be easy enough to get past, but Chalmers didn't like being this reliant on Umaren, let alone the seaplane captain's assessment of security.

The customs situation was unlike any he'd had to navigate, too. The downport required that any change in ownership or crew be reported to the authorities, but Umaren said they didn't bother to keep all that close a record of the comings and goings of the crews afterward. Indeed, they rarely checked incoming cargoes for contraband, which made sense in an odd sort of way. They had to be far more interested in outgoing traffic that might carry off some of the all-important drugs and medicines they were here to collect.

"Next!" the customs guy barked.

Umaren stepped forward and presented the customs officer with his documents, pretending a calm he didn't feel. Not from the sweat-slick fists he twined together behind his back, at any rate. Chalmers sidled closer, Jackson and Vizzel behind him.

"You never used to carry so many crew," the official said, thumbing through *Loklis'* manifest with one hand while he ran an eye over the men standing behind Umaren.

"The new owners wanted them aboard." Umaren leaned forward and added in a stage whisper meant to be heard by the crew, "I think to get rid of them. The owners have too many daughters who married men without other prospects." Chalmers and Jackson grumbled and tried to look more uncomfortable, playing their parts. Umaren continued, "They even said they're sending along another one in a few weeks."

"Well, if they want to cut down on the cargo you can carry, then that's their poor decision."

Umaren shrugged. "With the Sear nearly upon us, the new owners said they want to be sure we didn't look like an easy prize for pirates. Things are…not so stable as they usually are."

The official nodded. "Your new owners, what Brokerage?"

Umaren pointed at the paperwork. "Twin Star Trading, out of Kanjoor."

The official nodded, noting the name. "We've had a few new operations appear recently, what with the takeover of Whikmari Global Transport."

Umaren shrugged. "As you say. I just want to fly, and they pay on time."

The officer's condescending smile eased the knot of worry in Chalmers' gut. No one looked down that way on someone they considered a credible threat. It eased even further as the officer reached into a desk drawer and withdrew a stamp, which he then brought down on several successive pages of Umaren's paperwork.

"Next!" the official shouted as he gave Umaren a dismissive wave.

* * * * *

Seaplane

"You didn't tell me he'd be a giant. I'll need to offload some cargo just to carry his vastness," Umaren said quietly into the night wind.

Chalmers peered up the dock. A large man had entered the pool of light shed by the lantern at the seaplane's cargo hatch. Jackson and Vizzel had left it hanging there while they crammed the last few legitimate packages into the hold.

Chalmers recognized the "security specialist" from the photo included in the redacted files Murphy had furnished. Maximiliano Messina was certainly larger than most men but moved with the easy confidence Chalmers associated with dangerous people.

"Not with the lightweight parts we've been swapping into your plane these last weeks," Chalmers said. The replacement parts, mostly manufactured of ultralight and durable alloys, had been furnished by the SpinDogs. An old bootlegger's trick, that: removing and replacing all parts that weren't essential to a vehicle's speed and endurance and then tricking out the engines for maximum performance. Chalmers had insisted they dirty up the parts to make them look locally built, but any experienced mechanic who held one of the fuel pumps would know something was up. The work had freed up something on the order of five percent of the bulky, over-built seaplane's weight. More free weight meant either more product or better range per kilo of fuel.

Messina must have fixed their location before stepping into the light, as he walked straight toward Chalmers and Umaren, who stood in the deep darkness beside the crew door of *Loklis*.

"Messina," Chalmers said, extending his hand.

"Call me Moose, brother," the big man said, engulfing Chalmers' hand in one large paw. "Sounds more like an Indig name than my own."

"Sure, Moose," Chalmers said, wondering if he should have done something similar. Jackson easily got away with using his own name, as the locals took one look at him and assumed he was foreign to these parts.

Moose let his hand go without squeezing the life out of it and went to clasp Umaren's in turn.

There was a moment's fumbling as the local missed his first attempt at a grip, too busy looking up, and then up again, into Moose's eyes.

"Greetings, Captain Umaren. It is my honor to help protect you and your cargo on the ground."

"As I pledge to keep you safe in the air, Moose," Umaren said.

Umaren smiled and retreated into his beloved aircraft. He left the hatch open, the lights inside casting a wedge of light across the two Lost Soldiers.

"Damn," Chalmers said.

"What's that, Chief?" Moose asked, dropping into English for a moment.

"You sounded a lot more formal with the captain than I expected. According to your file, this is your first time on the surface. You do some research before coming down?"

"You bet. Pays to know your cultural cues. You know, in case someone wants to put a bullet in your—or my—head. Worked in-country, worked up there." He pointed skyward. "Should work here, too."

Chalmers started to laugh but was brought up short on recognizing the utter sincerity in the other man's eyes.

"Good point," he said. Looking for something to do to cover his awkwardness, he stooped to pick up the other man's bag. Or to try to. The thing was far heavier than Moose had made it seem.

Moose brushed his hand away without apparent effort. "I'll carry my weight and cover your six, Chalmers. You and the rest of the crew, that is."

"Good deal, Moose. I'll show you aboard. Not much elbow room, I'm afraid."

"Used to that after being up there," Moose said, following Chalmers through the hatch.

The plane dipped noticeably to the side as the big Lost Soldier climbed aboard.

*****

An Old Friend

Chalmers stepped off the plane onto a brand-new dock built expressly for *Loklis*. Made of fresh-sawn timbers that were already warping in the heat of the suns, it creaked in counterpoint to the gentle lapping of the waves on shore. Behind him, in no hurry to exit, Moose and Jackson were still arguing over the perfect BBQ technique: cut, spice, sugar, fat—the pair could argue for hours without coming close to a joint resolution. All they ever succeeded at was to either make Chalmers hungry or irritate him to no end. It was like the Student United Nations but less fun for Chalmers.

Chalmers stretched, enjoying the heat for a moment. What with the humidity off the sea, late afternoons at this latitude and with this wind were like a really, really hot day in Cabo. Finished stretching, he waved at the man reclining in the shade of a rather large pile of trade goods where the dock met the shore.

"Waiting long?" Chalmers called.

"Only since yesterday." The Lost Soldier's reply was in very, *very* good R'Bakuun. The coastal dialect Umaren and Vizzel had grown up speaking, no less. The man sat up, brushed sand from his robes, and waited for Chalmers to join him in the shade.

The paint made it hard to lock down, but something about the man struck Chalmers as familiar. *Not since making planetfall, but something else. Somewhere else. No, that wasn't it either.*

"You made good time, then," Chalmers said, extending his hand as he entered the shade.

The man took his hand in a firm, if slightly sweat-damp grip. "Murphy saw to it my goods and I were given priority. Lots to do and not much time to do it in."

"Right." Chalmers released the hand and waved at the crates, which were marked with the brokerage's twin stars. "To the efficient worker bee, more work."

"You calling me a drone?" the man asked, smiling under his paint.

Chalmers chuckled, shaking his head. "What should I call you?"

"Vat will do."

A cold thrill of recognition went through Chalmers, like ice water on hot pavement. He shivered. This was the same fucker CID had tasked Jackson and him with investigating when things went sideways in the Mog. The same fucker who'd been on the ill-fated Blackhawk with them. He'd had a single, blurry photo to work from back then, and, to be honest, his own problems had kept him from recognizing the former lieutenant of the US Army turned international arms dealer.

Fuck. That's where I recognize you from. You were on my book.

"You all right?" Vat asked.

"Yeah, just a little strung out from the flight," Chalmers said, hearing Jackson and Moose's heavier tread on the dock behind him.

"No you ain't. You recognized my name." Vat's eyes glittered with reflected light off the shallow lagoon.

Chalmers slowly rolled his shoulders, then cracked his neck. Finally decided, he said, "I was two steps behind you, back in the Mog."

"Oh?" The man's lips thinned, but he otherwise appeared relaxed, ready for anything. Butter wouldn't melt in this guy's mouth.

"Made a fair bit of trouble for me, you did."

Jackson walked up, did a double take. Moose had stopped somewhere out of sight.

"FBI sent over a team to get you," Chalmers said. "While they were with us, they got wind of some…irregularities in certain cases I had worked in the past."

"No shit?" Vat said.

"No shit."

"Well, sounds like you fucked up and got caught."

Chalmers bristled. Then, thinking of promises made and of the mission at hand, he reconsidered. A short, barking laugh escaped his lips. The humor came a bit more honestly after that first braying sputter—so much so that he folded over, hands on knees, to catch his breath when it was over. It was only then he realized that one of Vat's hands was concealed behind his thigh, holding something dark and metallic.

"Do we have a problem, Chalmers?" Vat asked, a feral look in his eyes.

"No, Vat, we don't. Not at all." He raised one finger. "I can't think of anyone better suited to this than the guy who kept ahead of us," he moved the finger in a circle to include Jackson and himself. "As well as the feebs for as long as you did."

The dangerous light dimmed. "Friend of mine stateside warned me they had me cold, were searching my home and business. That's why I was on the Blackhawk with you two. Trying to get out of Dodge before they caught me up. I had no idea the feds were already in Somalia."

"We good, Chalmers?" Moose asked.

Chalmers glanced at Jackson, who thought things through a moment, then nodded.

"We good, Moose. Just discussing a bit of shared history with our new friend Vat."

"Good deal. When do we eat?"

"They've got something barbequing. Smells amazing," Vat said, gesturing up the beach. "They've been smoking it all morning."

"Jesus, don't get them started on that," Chalmers said, smiling. He hadn't missed how, with the one hand distracting the viewer, Vat had used the other to make the pistol disappear into his clothing.

Jackson bought it, looked back from the cluster of low buildings on the foreshore only after Vat had empty hands.

"Nice pistol," Moose said.

"What pistol?" Vat asked, his hands as empty as his smile.

Chalmers snorted. "You're gonna fit right in, Vat."

* * * * *

Free Markets

"Didn't think they'd go in so hard for bloodsport," Chalmers said, taking in the ranked tiers of stone seats rising from the walls of the arena pit. The place could seat a *lot* of people.

"You're kidding, right?" Jackson said. "This kind of competition is just the kind of shit supremacists are into." He gestured at the arena as they walked down the aisle from the locker rooms the fighters used.

"Jackson's right," Vat said. "Given the way they are trained to think, it's quite natural to do this sort of thing. It ain't as popular out in the back country 'cause the satraps can't afford the wasted personnel and medical assets, but it turns out the lesser houses here are constantly looking for ways to prove themselves better than their neighbors without resorting to out-and-out warfare. Thus, the popularity of hand-fighting here among the brokerage personnel." He gestured at the stone ring at the middle of the building. Stretches of the sandy floor of the arena were still damp with blood from the evening before.

The group of Lost Soldiers made their way down onto the sands and stood looking up at the stands and private boxes. Both were empty.

"Looks expensive," Chalmers said, spinning on one heel to take it all in.

"It was," Vat said, outlining some blood with the toe of one sandal.

"Was?"

"Bought it last night." Vat said, looking him in the eye.

"I thought you said the owner refused your initial offer," Chalmers said.

Vat shrugged. "He did. And the second. I then made him an offer he couldn't refuse."

"Wake up with a horse head in his bed?" Moose asked.

Everyone turned to look at Moose, but it was Chalmers who blurted, "How do you know that reference?"

"What, just because I'm a big fella, I don't read?" the Vietnam-era Lost Soldier asked.

"Read?" Chalmers said, shaking his head. "It's a movie."

Vat started laughing first, then Jackson.

At last understanding dawned for Chalmers. "Right, the full title of the flick is *Mario Puzo's The Godfather*."

Moose blinked. "They made a movie out of the novel? Like *Gone With The Wind*?"

"Gone with th—" Jackson started.

"More, 'sleeps with the fishes' than 'gone with the wind!'" Chalmers cracked.

"Puzo co-authored the screenplay, even," Vat said, smiling at Moose.

Chalmers looked a question at him. The former arms dealer didn't seem the type to be a movie aficionado, but neither did he seem the type to be a mob boss.

Vat shrugged. "I watched that film a *lot*. Young James Caan was…very watchable."

Chalmers grinned and shook his head.

"I bet the book was better," Moose muttered in R'Bakuun, eyes roaming the stands.

"Must be an amazing novel…" Chalmers trailed off as he realized the big soldier's eyes were searching for threats. The exchange had been in English, and while they were supposed to be alone in here, there was always a risk someone was listening, and they were standing in an amphitheater designed to carry sound.

"Damn it," Chalmers said, in R'Bakuun. "We need to be careful."

The light mood of before was replaced by a moment's steady watchfulness from all of them. When no sounds or movement came from the cheap seats or the boxes, they all relaxed, if only marginally.

"But should you be pushing in on someone else's business like this?" Jackson asked quietly, breaking the watchful silence. "Won't it attract attention?"

Vat winced, half-shrugging. "The nature of this society makes some notice desirable, especially power-plays that are carried out with smooth authority. If it breaks no taboos or jeopardizes no one higher up the food chain, it gets me noticed. Notice means more access to power players and the opportunities they can provide. Combine this with my rapid rise to prominence on the merchant front, and people will start coming to me with information and for opportunities I might provide them."

Chalmers shook his head, toeing a darker patch of sand without thinking. His lip twitched in disgust as he realized it was blood.

Jackson was nodding, though. "Makes a sick kind of sense."

"Who brought the owner the offer he couldn't refuse?" Chalmers asked, careful not to look at Moose. He'd heard the security specialist had smoked a number of assassins bent on killing Murphy without breaking a sweat.

Vat met his gaze, held it. "Did it myself."

Uneasy, Chalmers changed the subject. "So, what's next?"

"I start playing for contracts serving the downport."

"We can do that?"

Vat smiled. "Brokers are *relied* on for that. The brokers here are considered more trustworthy than the individual members of the surveyors on some things. In their view, the humble R'Bakkuun are without Houses in the true Kulsian sense of the word, without a serious technological base of their own, and are therefore not considered any kind of *real* security threat. The brokers earn a living by facilitating the gathering of the biologicals before the Searing and then selling off whatever comparatively high-tech devices and goods the Kulsians leave behind as not valuable enough to freight back to Kulsis, give to their satraps here, or keep mothballed. Indeed, selling any real technology is more a black market activity than legitimate trade."

"Alright, so how do we use that?" Chalmers asked, resenting the other man's easy confidence.

"Why, we make nice with a broker or his minions, of course," Vat said, smiling.

*****

A New Friend

"Another delivery? I had thought Twin Stars had no more to give after being squeezed by Fangat," the clerk said, standing in the door of the Fangat warehouse. House Fangat held the Chair of the Broker Principle and wielded a *lot* of power. So much so their lowest employees seemed to think they could speak openly about Fangat's role in robbing a lesser brokerage like Twin Stars, even when they were only a warehouse manager, and about as far from the wealthy inner circle as Chalmers was from Earth.

"Yes, Daroz, another delivery of heavy, valuable goods from our good patron to yours," Jackson said, glancing at Chalmers as he and Moose wrestled the crate from the back of the truck.

Chalmers caught the look and stepped between the truck and the clerk. "Daroz, I have the thing you wanted."

"Not now, there is work to be done, you filth," Daroz said. The clerk was a waddling little punk with an inflated ego who felt that everyone should bow before his specialness. Unless, of course, someone of greater station appeared, at which point he behaved as if there were no more loyal or hard-working servants to be had in all the world. He was...thirsty, always looking to suck up to his betters or lord it over others. Of course the disappointment when his expectations met reality had proven a fine avenue to corrupting him.

Sweating in the incredible heat, Jackson and Moose set the crate down just inside the warehouse.

"My friend, you sure you don't want…" Holding the manifest in the same hand, Chalmers pulled a box the size of a cigarette pack from his breast pocket and shook a dull rattle from within as he handed both to the clerk.

"Well, I'll just check the manifest," the warehouse clerk said, licking his painted lips and taking the box from Chalmers. "I'll, umm, be back in a few minutes to sign off on everything."

Jackson shook his head as the guy hurried out of the warehouse, near salivating over his prize. A moment later Chalmers heard the faint clack of the latrine door closing behind the clerk. If previous experience was any judge, they had about fifteen minutes.

"Hope his need for the junk you're pushing doesn't get him removed or, worse yet, make him O.D.," Moose said, his bulk barely shadowing one corner of the vast warehouse door.

"Fuck Daroz," Jackson said, coming up behind the other man. "You didn't see him flog the shit out of a couple guys whose only crime was to drop a box. Didn't even break the contents, just dented the crate. That fucker had 'em whipped till they bled. Like that scene in *Roots*, man. I had flashbacks and shit."

"*Roots?*"

"Never mind. After your time. Probably not your jam anyway."

The sound of Moose's knuckles popping was like a sequence of slow, wet gunshots. "I suppose I prefer a more direct approach. Saw too many legs in-country get hooked on H to be comfortable with this kind of thing."

"Focus," Chalmers said, uneasy with it himself. It was all too easy—far too easy—to fall back into old habits. Shaking his head, he hiked a thumb at the crate sitting just inside the warehouse. "Get that in place, and I'll keep watch for our thirsty friend."

Jackson and Messina picked up the crate and carried it further into the darkened interior of the warehouse. The office was at the receiving end of the huge building. At the far end of the place the goods were transferred to cargo containers that were similar to CONEX boxes back on Earth: built to a regulation size, weight, and volume. The containers didn't leave the island but were commonly filled at warehouses outside the downport, so they had access to plenty of exemplars.

Chalmers did his part, lounging against the warehouse's office door and watching for the clerk's return. It had taken months of careful work to get to this point. If his pride in the job done thus far was wounded by the methods he had to use to accomplish the mission, it was a dull ache rather than the open sore he used to contend with. He shook his head. It still surprised him how much being honest to the people around him mattered. Yes, he had to lie like a rug, cheat, push drugs, do all manner of nasty shit, but doing it for the mission, for the Lost Soldiers' collective survival rather than for himself, made it somehow right. Like Murphy'd said, "Using your dark powers for good." He'd spent too much time like a rat, killing other rats just to get two more breaths on the sinking ship that was life. It was time to plug the hole that was sinking the ship, even if that meant swimming in some of the same old shit.

He started to pull at his lip but stopped with his hand halfway to his mouth. The sunblock paint jobs were a pain in the ass, but they did allow a certain amount of built-in disguise. That, and they were supposed to prevent skin cancer, an illness he wasn't eager to try on for shits and giggles. Not after watching his grandfather's nose get cut and re-cut to remove a tumor.

At least the paint—unlike so many sunscreens from his time—didn't smell like coconuts, which smelled like Malibu—the rum, not the place, which always summoned to mind a certain night puking his guts out in a Cabo gutter.

A rumble in the western sky announced a lighter on final approach. He resisted the urge to look at a watch he didn't wear while on the island and pretended a disinterested squint at the heavy security gate that kept the riffraff out of the downport proper.

The huge, angular craft thundered by high above the gates, held aloft by vastly-powerful engines as it slowed for landing and eased out of view below the fence line. Chalmers suppressed the urge to gape. He dragged his gaze from what was definitely some *Star Wars*-level shit back to the gate. None of the security contingent had even looked up. He'd have to look elsewhere for distracting the guards. Some were Kulsians, brought here on the first wave of ships. Those that weren't from off-world didn't want to get caught gawking.

Port traffic had steadily increased since his first visit with the crew of the *Loklis,* but, unlike his previous experience with smuggling, that increase in traffic had made security tighter, not more lax. He'd run the questionable behavior by Murphy, who'd asked their allies. The SpinDogs had a ready, if unwelcome, answer: the increased security measures were motivated more by the internal conflicts that so plagued Kulsian-style rule than by any real concern over threats posed by a given satrap or, more laughable still, the barbaric nomads. That was the reason they'd placed their downport here, so far from the mainland. It certainly wasn't convenient, but it was safe. An entire town of brokers and traders had grown up around the inner port. Not Kulsian, not satraps—they were a class unto themselves, sourcing and shipping those goods not seized outright by the reavers in the long lead-up to the Searing and then living off the proceeds in between.

Still, that they were so meticulous in guarding against internal threats meant problems for the operation. Penetrating the downport—he wanted to call it a starport, even though actual starships didn't land there—would be a lot harder than getting past security on the seaport. He'd tried to imagine how cutthroat Kulsian politics must be to generate such paranoia, but even films like *The Godfather* left him wondering if the mafia was paranoid *enough*.

The rumble of the lighter's drives eased back to a heavy drone and then ceased altogether. The security detail on the gate, a squad of painted men wearing what he'd been told was the grey of survey security uniforms, passed a small convoy of trucks onto the port property. Probably preparing to load the ship with cargo. The lighters usually took a day or two to refuel and prep, but they could speed that up in an emergency. It was pretty amazing when Chalmers thought about it. It had taken months for NASA to plan and execute shuttle launches into Earth's orbit, and here these assholes could turn a truly *interplanetary* ship around in a matter of hours. Probably less if they were in a real hurry.

"A hive of scum and villainy, indeed," he muttered.

"Just your kind of place, Obi-Wan," Jackson said from behind him.

"Who?" Moose said emerging from the shadows behind Jackson.

"Never mind," the partners chorused as the latrine door flew open. Daroz staggered when the door's rebound clipped his shoulder as he walked out into the light of both suns.

"Must be scratching that itch pretty good, Chalmers," Jackson murmured, nodding at the clerk, who had a dope-happy smile pasted across his face.

"Maybe too good," Moose said, equally quietly.

"He's where I want him," Chalmers muttered.

Coming to an unsteady halt, Daroz thrust the manifest back at Chalmers.

Seeing the signature crawled across the bottom, Chalmers bowed over it. "All is in readiness, Daroz," he said aloud, silently adding, *You thirsty fuck.*

"Then why are you still in my sight?" Daroz asked, dismissing them. He wheeled away to walk, loose-legged, back into his office.

"Mount up," Chalmers said, reflecting that some assets served best by being burned sooner rather than later.

* * * * *

Market Adjustments

"That's a bad sign," Jackson said, looking down from the balcony that ran around the upper stories of the Twin Star offices.

Chalmers nodded. Another crash sounded from below.

"Is it, though?" Vat said.

Jackson waved his hand. "That's like the third raid in the last two nights."

"Fifth, actually," Vat corrected. "The market is adjusting."

"The market?" Chalmers said.

Vat smiled. "We, well, *I* upset a few apple carts. No one likes price fixing, so they're regulating the market."

"But, haven't we been price fixing?" Jackson said.

"If anything, we've been undercutting the local market," Chalmers said.

"And we haven't been hit since the deliveries in the first week," Jackson added, looking thoughtful.

"You mean the deliveries I had—" Vat began.

"—you had *me* on a roundabout path through the docks," Jackson interrupted.

"And made sure no one but locals were with it when it got robbed," Chalmers added. Suspicion in full flame, he added, "And discussed at length with me at the fights."

"Yeah, those," Vat said. For some reason, the grin splitting his face reminded Chalmers of a shark.

"What was in the crates, Vat?" Jackson said, his tone telling Chalmers he had his suspicions.

"Oh, nothing much, just clear evidence that two of the most powerful brokerages have been engaged in artificial price-fixing to shore up their profits."

"But, those were our shipments, with Twin Star markings."

"Were they?" Vat asked, his grin becoming positively shit-eating. "Yes, they were marked for our warehouse, but the contents and the shipping manifests uniformly declared we were acting solely as shipping agents for Masok and Sons. What's more, all records indicate we were the middlemen for shipments between their mainland offices and Fangat Trading."

"I was wondering why we made a pay-off to Masok and Sons," Chalmers said. When Jackson sent an old-fashioned look his way, he shrugged, defensive. "I thought we were just kicking up a bribe to keep them off our backs."

"As far as anyone at Masok and Sons knew, it was," Jackson said, an edge of admiration creeping into his voice. "But to everyone else it looked like we were making good on their financial losses, confirming the evidence you gave them."

"Evidence of what?"

"Of collusion, naturally. Price fixing, more specifically. The only sin that counts here on the island." Vat's smile was no longer simply feral; it was positively beaming with pride. It somehow made his expression that much more malevolent.

"Jesus, man," Chalmers breathed. "That's some dangerous fire you're playing with."

"Not so dangerous, really." Vat shrugged, grin vanishing. "At least, not as dangerous as facing a motorized battalion of angry satrap goons."

Chalmers and Jacks shared a look at the apparent non sequitur.

Guess we all have our share of bad memories, Chalmers thought.

"But won't Twin Stars get spattered with the fallout?" Jackson said.

"Yes, but only in the sense that we will come out of this with some prize, some 'fallout ass,' I believe you breeder boys call it?" He grinned again. "Indeed, we should expect some representatives of the second tier brokerages to come by tonight or tomorrow, latest."

"What?" the partners chorused.

"I'm going to assume you understand what fallout is, and are wondering what the rest meant." Vat chuckled and gestured out beyond the balcony. "The middle and lower-tier brokerages are the ones pulling the raids on the primary houses. The ones who show up here tonight will likely know my play for a ruse, but also know it for a *very* useful ruse, one that allowed them to take direct action against the biggest brokerages without fear of reprisal from either the brokerages or the surveyors."

"Because they're all doing it, 'for the good of our collective reputation with the surveyors,'" Jackson breathed.

Chalmers glanced at his partner, stunned. Vat had done wonders to establish Twin Star Trading as *the* up-and-coming brokerage, to the extent the business was actually generating a profit, even without the regular influx of free goods from their allies on the mainland or the SpinDogs. The brokerage was now so large as to require a headquarters big and impressive enough to house the offices and critical employees of the organization, but this was an entirely different level of crazy.

"Jesus."

The doorbell rang. An old fashioned thing, it was an actual bell. On a rope.

Vat leaned back in his seat, his eyes glittering in the lamplight. "Someone want to get that for me?"

Chalmers and Jackson looked at one another. Neither one moved.

The bell clanged again.

"Moose!" Chalmers called.

"I got it, you lazy fucks," Moose stage-whispered from the hallway.

"Still, would have been nice for you to tell us your plans," Chalmers insisted.

Vat shrugged. "If you couldn't figure it out, from your position next to me, then I was sure the opposition couldn't follow the shell game I played."

"If I didn't know any better, I'd think you were enjoying this," Chalmers said.

"Oh, I *am* enjoying it. I mean, the more I'm here, the more I dig it. Cutthroat, sure, but everyone is so busy watching their opponents, they fail to see the board. I've earned—and spent—a king's ransom or two since we got to this island, and I'm getting ahead in a game I was not born to. All while being appreciated for my skills. What's not to like?"

"That and there's no one to keep you in line."

A murmur of voices from downstairs.

"No one?" Vat sniffed. "Shit, there's no *law*, just custom and power," Vat said. The erstwhile arms dealer's expression said he loved that lack.

"Just so long as you remember who your friends are, Vat," Jackson said, smiling to take the sting out.

Vat looked at him, did not smile back. "For all the bullshit, it's still straightforward to me: we're alone among enemies. Makes things very easy on the conscience."

Moose made some noise at the bottom of the stairs, said something apologetic and loud enough they were warned of his approach.

"I still think there's gonna be some violent pushback on this shit," Jackson said.

"And you didn't tell us the nuts and bolts of your plan. Kinda like a certain person we all know and love," Chalmers said, pointing skyward.

Vat frowned. "I'll ignore that aspersion for the moment to concentrate on my real reasons for keeping you all in the dark: when our shipment got hit on its way from the docks, would you have been able to *act* like you were as pissed as you really were?"

"Maybe," Chalmers said.

"Well, I wanted to be sure. We can't very well rely on maybes…" Vat said, trailing off as Moose escorted the broker's messenger into the room.

Chalmers bit back a retort. Knowing the logic backward and forward didn't make it feel any better to be the one duped.

The messenger bowed.

Vat's eyes flickered over the man's elaborate face paint. He must be reading it far faster than Chalmers could, because he immediately said, "Greetings, servant of Broker Thilokmes. What brings you here at this late hour?"

"Matters of import meant for your ears alone, Lead Broker Vat." The messenger looked at the others, haughty and dismissive.

Vat sat straighter, stared at the messenger. "You are not here to tell me who in my brokerage is worthy of trust, servant of Thilokmes. I will have you removed if you continue to behave so presumptuously."

Moose put a hand on one of the man's narrow shoulders and squeezed.

An audible swallow. "Apologies, Broker Vat."

Vat nodded acceptance of the apology and waited. Moose removed his hand from the man's shoulder.

"Thilokmes requests your backing in Council tomorrow. It is time the Fangat were ousted from the Chair of the Broker Principle. In return—" the doorbell rang again.

Moose glanced at Chalmers and smiled. The message was clear.

"In return?" Vat prompted.

Chalmers got up and started for the door.

"In return, he offers a waiver of fees to the amount of five percent of annual dues and duties."

"Five percent, eh?" Vat shook his head. "What Twin Stars requires is that five percent you mentioned in addition to preference for certain labor contracts—" Chalmers closed the door on the conversation and started down the stairs. The doorbell rang again before he'd made the landing. He sighed and wondered when they'd all become Vat's servants.

*****

High Noon

"Down!" Moose hissed.

For once, Chalmers did what he was told. Of course, some of his compliance was the result of Moose's off-hand wrapping itself around the nape of his neck and shoving him into a shambling, hunched run across the tiles of the market square.

Gunfire rattled from behind them, punctuated by the sound of rounds crackling against stone.

Jackson was already well ahead of Chalmers, sliding the last few steps to halt in the dubious shelter of the large fountain dominating the center of the square.

Chalmers glimpsed Moose aiming the fifteen-millimeter pistol he preferred back the way they'd come. Despite being aware it was coming, Chalmers still jumped as Moose's weapon barked, then barked again.

Chalmers fled in a crouch that, within a few panicked strides, fetched him up next to Jackson in the lee of the fountain's basin. Moose followed after, slow and precise with each shot, letting the big pistol fall back on target before squeezing off the next round as he marched in their wake.

He looked from the big shooter to his partner. Jackson's light pistol, a local-made job he and Chalmers carried to better fit in, had appeared in his hand.

Chalmers pulled his own pistol, wishing he'd spent more time with it at the range.

"Fucking Vat! 'Fangat won't dare strike at us,' he says!" Jackson snarled, firing at the men on the east side of the square. Men whose faces were painted in the grey-barred blue of the Fangat Brokerage.

At least no bystanders were going to get plugged. No one who did not absolutely have to be was out and about at noon on R'Bak during the Searing. Chalmers wouldn't have been, either, if there hadn't been a minor emergency at the arena. They'd been on their way home from putting out that fire when Moose had seen the armed men approaching. Which was, on reflection, probably part of the trap that had been laid for them.

Chalmers discarded thoughts of how the trap had been set up in favor of getting free of it. He looked around, assessing their situation. They were just over two blocks west of the Twin Stars offices. Things would be over long before any help could arrive from that quarter. The square was about thirty meters on a side, with the fountain sheltering them in the middle. The ambusher's plan appeared to have been well-timed to isolate the Lost Soldiers, but they appeared to have traded isolating their victims for allowing their prey access to cover. Unless…He glanced over the rim of the fountain. The men that had triggered the ambush were no longer advancing; they were now either trying to find cover along the edges of the square or already in it. Chalmers turned, put his back to the fountain and looked up just as a pair of armed men rose from the roofline.

"Fuck! Six, high!" he shouted, raising his pistol. It was a long, shitty shot at this range, one Chalmers didn't think he could make on a good day. He banged a couple rounds that way anyway, just to keep them honest.

One figure ducked, overbalanced, slid on the tile rooftop, and fell, arms wind milling. A brief, wordless scream was cut short when his head made its inevitable, heavy, wet crunch into hot stone tiles. The dead man's gun hit the tiles stock-first an instant later. Something must have broken in the firing mechanism on impact, because the gun discharged uselessly into the white-hot sky.

"Nice!" Moose thumped down against the wall of the fountain next to him, reloading. "Keep 'em thinking about their skin, snake!"

Unsure why Moose was calling him a snake, Chalmers nodded and squeezed two more rounds at the remaining guy above them. He didn't hit a damn thing. The ten-millimeter light pistols carried more rounds than the bigger fifteen-millimeter that Moose carried, but the barrel length of both weapons made for shit accuracy at this range.

Jackson's pistol crack-cracked, hammering his eardrums. Wincing, a distracted Chalmers couldn't help but grin as Moose moved. The big man looked a little ridiculous crab-walking below Chalmers' extended arms and around Jackson's back to take up a position opposite where he'd taken cover.

"When I pop up and fire, move to the plants over there, copy?" Moose's shouted English was accompanied by a gesture of his free hand toward the narrow road that entered the west side of the square.

Chalmers looked and saw a big planter box about a third of the way between their present position and the road that let off the square. Part of a border for the night-time seating area of a cafe in that side of the square, the plants rising from it had definitely seen better days.

"Copy!" the partners shouted.

Water splashed on Chalmers' shoulder as bullets were swallowed in the basin behind him. He looked up to see the guy on the rooftop standing to get a better angle on the three Lost Soldiers below. Chalmers aimed, fired. The shooter flinched behind some ornamental stonework.

"Red!" Jackson shouted, dropping into full cover to reload.

Chalmers shot again at the man above, turned on his shoulder, and, not even bothering to aim, sent a few rounds in the general direction of the men on the far side of the square.

"Up!" Jackson shouted, shooting again even as Chalmers' slide racked back and stayed there.

"Red!" Chalmers yelled, fumbling for the magazine next to his holster.

"Go! Go! Go!" Moose said in nearly the same instant, rising from his position and resuming his almost metronomic fire.

Someone screamed at the other end of the square.

Jackson popped a few off at the man on the roof and started toward the dubious safety of the planter.

"Fuck!" Chalmers gasped, staggering to his feet. He stumbled along in Jackson's wake, trying to jam the fresh magazine home in his weapon and screaming silently at the device, wondering why *the fuck* it wouldn't succumb to the desperate power of his need. Belatedly realizing he wasn't using the Beretta he'd trained on for years, he finally found the magazine release a finger's breadth up from where it should be. He dumped the spent mag with a metallic clatter and slapped the fresh one home. He was just looking up when something slewed him around by his belt and tossed him into the cover of the planter box.

"Scratch one," Moose growled as another scream sounded.

Chalmers looked up, saw Moose standing over him, firing again. The man had somehow seen Chalmers was out of it, dragged him back and pushed him to cover, all without losing track of—or missing—his target.

Jackson was shooting back the way they'd come, too. "One mag left."

"One here," Moose said. "And then my hold-out."

"I've got…the one in my gun," Chalmers said, watching the roofline. The Lost Soldiers had moved closer to that side of the square. With any luck, it would force the shooter up there to stand and expose more of himself to get an angle on them.

"Cover me," Moose said, taking a knee to reload.

Chalmers turned and, seeing movement, cracked a few shots at a man charging toward the fountain they'd abandoned. The guy went down with an angry cry, though Chalmers didn't think he'd scored a hit. He wasn't happy with that result. The charging man meant that group was advancing again. Probably because the rooftop men had failed to put rounds in Chalmers and friends and end the fight.

Chalmers' shots must have got the attention of the man's companions, because the desiccated growths rising from the planter above it started shivering as bullets whickered through dried out fronds and whacked into trunks. Pottery shattered as bullets clattered into, and through, the far side of the planter.

Chalmers cowered lower behind the planter and gave a silent but fervent prayer of thanks for the potter, the gardener, and every other person who might have played a part in causing the planter to be here, protecting his sinner's carcass in this moment of peril. He turned, wide-eyed, to tell Moose the good news, but he'd dropped so low that Moose's pistol, held at his own knee, was at his eye-level for what happened next.

Moose's huge hand finished seating a fresh magazine and let the slide forward into battery. Looking up from the gun and hands, Chalmers saw the big veteran wasn't looking his way. Instead, Moose was looking up over one round shoulder. He followed the line of Moose's gaze and saw the rooftop shooter come into view again.

The man leaned out to draw a bead on Chalmers.

Everything slowed down. He blinked, tried to raise his own gun. It was heavier than worlds, and dragged against Chalmers' every effort to bring it into line.

Chalmers watched in slow-motion as, still on one knee, still looking up at the shooter over his shoulder, Moose calmly pushed his pistol under his free arm and, muzzle barely protruding from beneath the armpit, pulled the trigger. The pistol barked, hot brass tinkling off the planter to sizzle painfully against Chalmers' cheek.

The man on the rooftop stood straight, a red strain spreading from the center of his torso. He fell, only to end up hanging by the scarf he wore as the thick fabric caught on something. His blood didn't so much drip as click, almost entirely dry before it hit the seared ground.

Moose snorted. "Never in a million years."

Late, Chalmers' own pistol barked, bullets sparking against the wall beside the swinging body.

Time seemed to unlock, wind out faster and faster, almost to normal speed again. Jackson was shooting again, the sound driving more pain into his skull.

Moose yanked Chalmers to his feet, pushed him toward the road again. The deeper bark of his pistol sounded a few more times as the partners staggered into the shade of the buildings framing the road off the square.

"Keep going," Moose panted. "They're done, for now."

They crossed the few blocks in a paranoid, blurred, sweaty rush. It was only when he cramped up in the relative shelter of the office that Chalmers realized not a one of them had complained about the heat since the shooting started.

* * * * *

Fresh Orders

Exceedingly bored and a little warm, Chalmers leaned back and yawned. Things had been pretty calm since the attempted assassination a few weeks back, and he'd never found paperwork exciting. Awareness had faded into a light doze when the office door slammed open. Jackson entered and winged a message packet across the desk at him. Chalmers ducked. The packet bounced from the wall behind him and to the ground.

"What the hell!" Chalmers said.

Jackson snorted.

"Seriously, you sick bastard. What do you think it is?" Chalmers bent to pick up the packet.

"I suspect we're getting fresh orders," Jackson said. He was grinning as Chalmers sat upright from collecting the packet from the floor.

Ignoring the letter opener lost somewhere under the papers scattered on his desk, Chalmers pried the packet open with his thumbnail.

He flipped through several pages, then sorted them in the proper order. He removed the code book—a very real technical manual on aircraft engines—from the desk and flipped it open. It took a minute and some absent-minded cursing, but Chalmers eventually had the headline deciphered.

"Operation BUCKET," he read aloud. "What the hell is BUCKET?"

"Won't know 'till you decrypt the rest, genius."

Chalmers sat back. "I freely admit you're better at this than I am, Jacks."

"Damn straight I am, but it's your turn." He looked thoughtful a moment. "Bucket like an old car, maybe?"

"We won't know until the resident genius decodes it," Chalmers said, but he was grinning as he picked up the manual.

The grin died a quick death as he dove into decoding the rest of the message. Dimly, he noted that Jackson sat still and silent while he worked, giving his partner both time and quiet in which to work. A quiet only broken by his own occasional expletive as the new orders were slowly, painfully revealed.

"Fuck me," he breathed once he'd finished.

"What?" Jackson asked, leaning forward and trying to read upside down.

"Murphy wants us to play *Ice Pirates*!"

"What?" Jackson said.

Chalmers looked at his partner. "A SF flick. Eighty-three or f—"

"Why'd you make him black?" Jackson interrupted, doing a fair impression of Robert Urich.

Chalmers sat back in his chair, surprised his partner knew the movie.

"'Cause I wanted him to be perfect,'" Jackson quoted, as if reading from a film script. "It's an immortal line for black SF fans. Roscoe was the shit. And the black robot made the movie. So, yeah, I know the fucking flick, Chalmers." He shook his head and flipped the decoded message around to read for himself. "I meant, what, specifically, does Murphy want us to do?"

"He wants us to capture a lighter intact. Preferably without alerting the rest of the port that it's been taken."

Still reading, Jackson sat back in his chair and muttered, "Not asking for much, is he?"

Chalmers grinned. "Never."

"Says here we're to rendezvous for further instruction. There's also a schedule for delivery of additional assets beginning next month…" Jackson let his voice trail off, shaking his head.

"And he adds that we should prepare preliminary plans for review," Chalmers finished for his partner.

Jackson let the hand holding the orders fall into his lap. "The guys are not going to be happy, being forced to leave after all the work they've put in."

"Unless we can pull it off without revealing our hand," Chalmers said, pulling his lip.

"We need Vat's thoughts on this. Where is he?" Jackson asked. He'd already forgiven Vat for underestimating the violent response of Fangat.

"Meeting with the Ghnzi," Chalmers said, lip curling. He, on the other hand, had yet to forgive the former arms dealer for underestimating the backlash from Fangat over the Broker Principle position.

"Moose with him?"

"Yeah."

"Send a messenger to ask him to come back to the office?"

"No." Chalmers shook his head. "Not that time critical, really. We can get started without him."

Jackson was looking across the papers at him, expression showing he saw right through Chalmers' bullshit.

"I'll just send someone to make sure he comes straight here instead of the baths or his club," Jackson said in the tone that told Chalmers it wasn't up for discussion. Setting the papers on the desk, Jackson stood up and left the office.

Wanting to distract himself, Chalmers set about clearing the desk for action. That done, he bent and uncovered the floor safe containing sensitive documents. Entering the combination, he withdrew a bundle of files containing hand-drawn maps and hastily-written patrol schedules. Each had been cajoled out of compromised personnel—confirmed by first-hand observation by a Lost Soldier where possible—then collated and constantly updated over months of painstaking surveillance work. He pinned each piece of the puzzle to the local version of a cork-board, and had to set up another one to take all the material. He was just finished laying it all out when Jackson returned.

Seeing their work in plain view, Jackson quickly closed the door behind himself. The brokerage employed a substantial number of local hires, and while they were as loyal as could be expected, that particular bar was set at about knee height.

"Security is tight," Chalmers muttered, examining the most recent guard schedule for the main gate.

"And we were focused on sabotage—getting access to fuel lines and the parts depot—thinking that's what Murphy would want," Jackson said, leaning on the desk with both hands.

"Vat was right, though," Chalmers admitted grudgingly. "The Kulsians are focused on internal competition, not infiltration by outsiders hostile to their presence."

"Can you blame them? What back-country R'Bakuun madman could get across the ocean, then past their security—and then, what could such a relative primitive accomplish if, by some miracle, they managed a breach?"

Chalmers cocked his head. "Terror attacks?"

"And not much more."

"Yeah, this mission might be more easily accomplished than it sounds."

Jackson snorted. "You been smoking that shit you give Daroz? Last I checked, we barely qualified with space suits. I sure as hell don't know the first fucking thing about piloting a spacecraft."

"Me neither, but I gotta believe Murphy has something planned," Chalmers said.

"A SpinDog pilot?"

"Could be. Or maybe one of us Lost Soldiers underwent Doorknob training before they bounced?"

"It's Dornaani, you dick," Jackson said.

"I know that. Not like any of those assholes are around to correct me. They took off, so I figure we don't owe 'em shit." Chalmers shook his head. "What I was trying to say before you so rudely interrupted me, was that the mission might be both easier and harder than it looks."

"How so?"

"The perimeter security is hard, sure, but once past the gates and fences almost everything is focused on keeping their own side from stealing cargo. Their measures against outsiders are almost laughable in comparison."

Jackson slowly nodded, understanding dawning in his eyes. "So they won't be on the lookout for someone to trying to stow away."

Chalmers felt the hair on his arms stand up, a sure sign they were either onto something big or his thinking was entirely, even idiotically, wrong.

Only time would tell which was correct.

*****

Damaged Goods

"Everything all right?" Vat said upon entering the office.

Chalmers was glad to see Moose shadowing the smaller man. He waved him in as well.

"Sort of," Chalmers said, closing the door behind Moose.

"What's up?" Vat said, glancing from Jackson's pensive expression to Chalmers' poker face as he stepped across the icebox set in the wall. There wasn't any ice in it, but rather the broken branches of a particular plant that had an intense endothermic reaction when submerged in a particular solution of water and a honey-analogue of all things.

"New orders," Chalmers said.

"So?" Vat pulled a pitcher of blespa juice from the fridge and poured himself a drink. Keeping hydrated in the growing heat was a stone bitch, even if you were only outdoors for a short while.

"So, the objective is so high-value it—or the aftermath of acquiring it—might require us to cease all other operations on the island. Indefinitely."

Vat's knuckles whitened as he clenched his fist around the glass. "What?"

Moose had to turn sideways to get by Chalmers and take the pitcher from Vat. He poured himself a glass. "Anyone else?" he offered.

"No, thanks," the partners chorused.

"Answer the question, Chief," Vat said tightly.

"I heard you," Chalmers said, intentionally omitting the other man's rank. Vat was, ostensibly, his superior, but this op was so far off the regs as to be undetectable to the naked eye. Besides, using ranks was a dead giveaway to eavesdroppers that they weren't who they appeared to be, so he was covered.

"So." Vat set his glass down on the sideboard with a dull thunk and crossed his arms. "You gonna keep us in suspense?"

Chalmers shook his head. "First, I want to tell you I want to keep going as we have almost as much as you do. I enjoy the trappings of power here, too."

"What the fuck is the target?" Vat growled.

"It's just that I know you're a little too happy here, enjoying your wealth and whatnot," Chalmers said, knowing he was winding the other man up but unable to help himself. "The challenge, that kind of thing, to your skills."

"I don't need this shit," Vat said, turning to leave.

"This about stealing the lighter?" Moose asked, looking at Jackson.

"Sure is," Jackson said, then he looked at Moose, eyes wide.

Everyone in the room turned to look at Moose, who chose that moment to chug his drink.

"You knew?" the partners chorused.

"Steal a lighter?" Vat sputtered at the same time.

"I did," Moose said to Jackson and Chalmers. "And," he continued, looking across at Vat, "yeah, it was part of the plan from the first sign of the surveyors approaching."

"Wait," Chalmers said. "Why tell you and not us?"

"Because you and Jackson might have been caught and tortured in the early days of the operation. So. Here's to that not happening." Moose lifted his glass and pretended clinking it with another. "And, if we were cut off from reaching higher, I was to inform you of the mission if a month passed absent fresh orders from on high."

"But why keep it from me, then?" Vat said.

Chalmers almost sneered, hearing the incredulity in Vat's voice.

"I'm not sure, but I do have a lengthy record of keeping my mouth shut and my nose clean while I *follow* orders." He looked meaningfully from Chalmers to Vat, the silent subtext clear to both: *And I don't dick around on a mission. Ever.*

Jackson shook his head. "Shit."

"Well," Vat said. "I ain't playing this go-round. Not if it means sacrificing everything I built, again."

"I?" Chalmers said. "There's no 'I' in team, buddy."

"Like you could've done this without me, you redneck fuck."

Chalmers came off the door. "Who you callin' redneck, yo—?

"Murphy plays a damn deep game," Jackson said, loud enough that his voice cut across Chalmers' retort.

"*Has* to," Moose said, nodding.

"What's that?" Chalmers snarled.

"Murphy *has* to play hardball." Moose looked at each of the other men in turn. His normally placid expression was displeased, even angry.

"Look, the shit I did up in orbit? The stuff that made it politically expedient to send me down here? Well, it wouldn't have been necessary if the political situation up there weren't clear as mud. Right when everything was going well for us planetside, when we had the J'Stull satraps on the run, that's when the factionalism among the SpinDogs started getting murderous." He sighed. "No, that's not right. The factions became even *more* murderous then."

He shook his head. "But that's not really my point." He jabbed a finger at Chalmers and then Vat. "You two take every command in light of how it affects you, personally. Makes you feel like the decisions Murphy is making are meant to dick with you, personally. I'm here to tell you that attitude is complete bullshit, and a product of your misapprehension that the fucking universe revolves around you, gives a fucking *shit* about you, about any one of *us*. Thinking it's personal in any way is wrong. So fucking *wrong*.

"I had the opportunity to watch Murphy work up there. Every *single* decision he makes is intended to increase our collective chances of survival. Not his personal power or individual odds of survival, mind you. He could have easily secured a position of relative security for himself with the SpinDogs by using up the Lost Soldiers like so many bullets in his sidearm. He hasn't—*he won't*—do that because he's trying to ensure our survival. Not his, not mine, not any single one of us, but our *collective* survival. And in deciding to do that, he's been repeatedly forced to bet on our skills and our will to win to even the odds in a brutal, zero-sum game that we either persevere in or perish from."

A thoughtful silence fell as the big man stopped speaking.

Vat was looking at his hands, face twisted as if he were in pain.

Chalmers had never been one to feel much shame, but he felt his cheeks burning under Moose's accurate assessment of his shitty attitude. What made it even more painful was that Chalmers was sure that if he were to add together the word count of every conversation Moose had taken part in since the big guy had joined them, the sum wouldn't equal half the words he'd just spoken. More than that, he'd never heard Moose express an opinion, positive or negative, on anyone in their little ersatz unit. He'd consistently presented a uniformly solid workman's attitude to getting the job before him done and a sly sense of humor that was fun, if not as edged as Chalmers' and Jackson's could be.

For the first time in a long time he thought about his vow to do better, to be better, and how he might have fallen short of that in front of his peers, especially recently.

"Still waters run deep," Jackson breathed, breaking the silence.

"That they do," Vat said, looking at Moose first and then Chalmers.

"Look man, I shouldn't have been trying to push your buttons," Chalmers said, recognizing the moment.

"And I shouldn't have called you a redneck," Vat said.

Chalmers shrugged. "Shoe fits and all…"

"Damn, brother, you know how to cut through the bullshit." Jackson reached out and offered his hand to Moose, who clasped it, then drew the smaller man in for a rib-thumping pat on the back.

"Now we got all the bitching, moaning, hugging, and groaning out the way, can we get on with the business at hand?" Moose said, gesturing past Jackson at the map-and-report-littered boards.

* * * * *

Conference

"Don't forget to use the code words for everyone," Jackson reminded Chalmers for what seemed like the tenth time since they landed.

"I won't, thanks." He shook his head. "The time delay'll make this a stone pain in the ass." Chalmers gestured at the communications unit's readout, which listed the current delay at thirteen minutes, thirty-seven seconds, and some change. One thing about the universe Chalmers and the other Lost Soldiers had found themselves in: some laws of physics were a lot more in the realm of *2001: A Space Odyssey* rather than *Star Wars: A New Hope.*

"It's still quicker than what we have in town. We could be filling out codes and shit back on the island and waiting weeks on the communications loop to close," Jackson said. He smiled, added quickly, "Then again, we're gonna have to inform the rest of the crew what's expected of us. I'm sure that'll be *tons* of fun."

The communications unit was SpinDog manufacture and used a tight beam antenna set in a cleft up the draw from where the bunker was sited.

Chalmers nodded, girded his loins with his robes and sat down on one long side of the table the mic sat on. The spartan communications bunker they occupied was buried well up in the hills above the beach, concealed in a crease in the rock that would be subject to flash floods when the Searing was over, but remained dry as a bone as the Searing approached. While spartan, it was far cooler inside than out. It reminded him of trips to Vegas, the way the temperature dropped thirty degrees on entering a building. He didn't know if they kept the place cool for the people who used it or the communications gear itself. Probably the latter.

"Five gets you twenty he says 'bottom line' in the first five minutes," Chalmers said as the countdown went into single digits.

"With or without the delay?"

"Shit, wi—no, without!"

Jackson grinned. "That's a bet, Chalmers."

The comm chirped, the light indicating a connection started to glow.

Chalmers clicked the mic on. "PRIMARY is present. Coded assessment of capabilities of WORMWOOD transmitting. Parameters for BUCKET received and verified by SECONDARY. TERTIARY believes there is a window of opportunity to accomplish the mission. TERTIARY convinced PRIMARY and SECONDARY of same, but all of us agree that the mission objective is undeliverable barring additional assets." Which was an understatement. None of them had suddenly developed the skills necessary to fly—was it fly? No, operate—a damn lighter.

The comm panel chirped, additional lights indicating both the verbal and written messages had been sent.

Chalmers clicked the mic off. He kicked back, putting his thick-soled sandals up on the table while they waited for a response. Jackson did the same on the other side of the table.

Chalmers hadn't been a fan of sandals before R'Bak. Seemed they were a recipe for sunburn on some really sensitive skin. Or, worse yet, bug bites. But near the tropics of R'Bak, where the sun seemed to delight in making leather boots an oven, he'd been happy enough to ditch the uniform and don the sandals, especially since the local equivalent of walking-about clothes was either body paint for a laborer or thick, stifling robes for the merchant-gentry. The latter at least kept the feet from being exposed, and let some air circulate on them.

"Think he'll update us on Elroy?" Jacks asked, drawing Chalmers from his contemplation of footwear and proper dress codes.

Chalmers shook his head. "Doubt it. Murphy's not one to gossip, especially on a mission."

"Can you ask?"

"Of course," Chalmers said, lacing his fingers behind his head.

Jackson fixed him with a glare made less venomous by coming between their sandals across the table.

"What?" Chalmers said, hating the defensive note his voice held.

"Man, you don't get to say it like that. All cool and shit. Not with the way you were on the radio when he was on mission."

Chalmers dropped his hands, was about to defend himself when the comm went live. "PRIMARY, we applaud your team's achievements thus far. Operation BUCKET's last remaining piece, MENDACITY, will be arriving in three weeks, coordinates coded in the accompanying transmission. Bottom line, MENDACITY will make BUCKET deliverable. Caution in employment of MENDACITY advised. Please stand by as we integrate your most recent reports with other operational data and advise."

"Jesus," Jackson breathed, letting his chair thump back on four legs.

"What, pissed you lost the bet?" Chalmers said.

"No, of course not. Mendacity not mean anything to you?"

"Should it?" Chalmers said, flogging his vocabulary for the term.

Jackson shook his head, wonder writ large on his features. "How you crackers ever came to rule the world, I'll never understand. Can't even be bothered to read a goddamn dictionary. Your *own* goddamn dictionary, at that."

"It's just a code word," Chalmers said, wishing Jackson would let slip what the word actually meant.

"Sure, buddy. You would think that. Mark my words, man: this bodes ill."

"Since when did you start dropping words like, 'bodes?'" Chalmers asked.

"What, don't know what that one means, either?"

"Fuck you, Jacks," Chalmers said, grinning. "Sounds like whoever MENDACITY is, they'll require watching, but have the skills necessary for BUCKET?" He could see several ways that could go horribly wrong, up to and including acting like they were with the program right up until the lighter was taken, then betraying the whole operation to the surveyors.

"Right…a SpinDog?"

"Can't think of anyone else with the necessary skills."

"Someone from the wrong side of the recent unpleasantness Moose was talking about?"

"Must be…shit, we don't know, and won't even have a chance to formulate our opinion until the fucker arrives." He glanced over at the coordinates the tech had up on his screen. "At least we'll be picking them up at Fibberzs Bay on the way to Kanjoor. Convenient, if long, flight path."

"That's great. Just great," Jackson groused.

"What?"

Jackson shook his head. "Crack a goddamn dictionary, would you?"

"What?"

"We'll be picking up a guy code-named 'lying' at a place that translates into English, phonetically, as, 'Little Liar's Bay!'"

"Shit," Chalmers said, connecting the dots between the words now that Jackson had painted the lines clearly. "When you put it that way, it really does sound bad. Think Murph is trying to tell us something?"

"Ya think?"

Chalmers thought about that and his obligation to promises already made. Deciding on how to word what he was about to say, he set his sandals on the floor and keyed the mic.

"We will pay close attention to MENDACITY to ensure success of BUCKET. While we wait for you to digest reports regarding BUCKET, PRIMARY wants to know if THE KING has recovered."

"THE KING?" Jackson said.

"Now who's showing his ignorance?"

Jackson grimaced, flipped Chalmers the bird.

"Pretty sure Elroy means, 'the king' in French. Creole or something."

"No shit?"

"No shit," Chalmers said. After a minute staring at the comm, he got up, made himself a drink, and spent a few minutes watching the readout as the data Murphy was sending trickled in. Unable to make sense of it without more and better context, he took his sweet time returning to his seat, just to find that only a couple minutes had passed. He sighed and mumbled, "This is the worst."

"Nope. Still better than manually coding shit," Jackson said, leaning back in his chair again.

Chalmers pretended to toss that idea in the shitter, even flushed after.

Jackson grinned. "Thanks for asking, Chalmers."

"No sweat, man. I hope he's better."

They waited in a more comfortable silence. The large fan that served the bunker's heat-pump kicked on. The air grew noticeably cooler. Chalmers savored the sweet cool air across his toes.

The comm clicked on. "THE KING is doing better than expected, but still has to defeat a few rebels," Murphy said. "We will reestablish contact in eighteen hours with further direction in light of WORMWOOD success and possible targets for BUCKET. End transmission."

"Since we're here another day, want to get the rods out? See if we can't catch something edible for dinner?"

"Probably won't be able to eat most of what we might catch, but sure." Chalmers shrugged, dreading the heat, but content to be doing anything other than stressing over what was to come.

*****

Mendacity

"He doesn't look special," Umaren said, voice pitched to carry over the roar of the engines as the seaplane turned to shore and the dock.

Chalmers, crammed into the space between the pilot and co-pilot, and trying not to hit anything important, squinted at the figure emerging from the trees on the foreshore. Unable to make out dick for details and unwilling to admit it, he simply nodded at the pilot and stepped back into the small gangway between cockpit and cargo bay.

Now that the plane was plowing through the water, the late afternoon suns began to heat her interior faster than the cooling system could rid the hull of heat. Chalmers was sheathed in sweat by the time he'd eased his way past some of the goods they'd picked up in Kanjoor and made it to the water cargo hatch. He plugged his headset into the intercom system and opened the small porthole set in the cargo hatch. Hot, humid air began to puff into the seaplane. It didn't do much to cool him off, even standing in front of the opening.

"Man, it's fucking hot! Crack a window, Umaren!" Chalmers barked.

"Wouldn't have to if you hadn't insisted on stripping her biggest cooling units to make room for your contraband!" Umaren snapped.

"Contraband that's made you wealthy beyond your wildest dreams," he said, sweating. The words were Umaren's own, or close enough. The pilot and his partner had appeared at a Twin Stars soirée in Liberace-level outfits. When asked to tone it down a bit, Umaren had claimed such conspicuous display was necessary to convey their undreamed of level of success.

He felt a strong draft of—if not cool, then at least fast-moving—air as the pilot opened one of the cockpit windows.

"Thank you, Umaren," he said with heartfelt sincerity.

Chalmers spent the next few minutes twisting and turning to cool various body parts in the artificial breeze. That had to stop when Umaren slowed the seaplane even further for the final few yards to the docks. The heat quickly rose to sweltering again, but, not wanting to flood the plane with an errant wave, Chalmers waited for the command from Umaren to unbutton.

"Make secure," Umaren said a sweaty minute later.

Chalmers undogged the hatch and pushed the upper half up just as they pulled alongside the dock. He reached out and cast a line across a convenient bollard, making the toss the first time, despite the prop wash. He smiled. He'd never have been so good with a rope just six months past. Hell, he'd not known a tenth of the nautical and aviation vocabulary—in English or R'Bakuun—he used on a weekly basis when they'd started this op.

"Starboard roped," he said.

"Bow roped," Vizzel reported from the bow hatch, just forward of the cockpit.

"Secure," Umaren said. A moment later the engines died, props slowly spinning to a halt.

In the relative silence that descended, heat expansion summoned the occasional ping from the upper hull, a counterpoint to the gentle lapping of wavelets on the lower hull.

Chalmers looked at the shore. The vegetation that ringed the lagoon had thinned, grown ragged and dry, offering far less foliage than just a few weeks ago. It looked a little like some Vietnam-era photos he'd seen of stretches of jungle hit with Agent Orange.

Taking a long pull of water from his canteen, Chalmers dropped the lower half of the hatch to rest on the dock. He returned the canteen to his belt. The blaze of snow-white paint covering the interior of the hatch was blinding in the light. He blinked and walked off the seaplane onto the dock. Standing still in direct sunlight was brutal, but it was so hot he might pass out if he exerted himself more than maintaining a slow walk. He looked longingly at the lagoon, but knew it wouldn't be much of a relief, either. The shallow water wasn't that much cooler than the air here along the border of the tropics. Besides, seawater would melt the paint protecting his skin faster than sweat and he couldn't afford the sunburn two minutes of direct sunlight would give him if his protective coating thinned, let alone washed off completely. He had a growing hotfoot going by the time he cleared the dock and approached the man standing among the native vegetation.

As instructed, the paint on Mendacity was plain white, ready for Umaren to embellish with crew markings. The paint also made it hard to tell what the guy looked like beyond the even facial features and hard golden eyes. That took Chalmers aback a moment. Upon reading the section of Murphy's file describing the man's eye color, Chalmers had assumed an error. But no, the man's eyes were really gold. They also had that hard edge Chalmers had learned to associate with people who'd been in the shit a little too often and left there a little too long for safety's sake.

Chalmers came to a stop a few feet from the other man. He did not extend a hand, and waited for Mendacity to speak first, reflecting that the mind games these people played on meeting one another for the first time were far less "sniff the other dog's ass" as "must show them who's boss from the get-go."

A brief hesitation, then the man spoke. "I am Yukannak. You are Chalmers?"

"I am."

A deep bow. "I am at your service."

"I have your word on that?" Chalmers said, watching the other man's painted face very closely. According to his file, he was a renegade Kulsian who had played both ends against the middle quite smoothly in the recent past, and, while Chalmers admired a good player as much as the next guy, it was his ass if Yukannak decided he could score a better deal with the opposition in the next few weeks.

"I have given my word to your Colonel Murphy," the man said. "I give it to you."

Good poker face, Chalmers thought.

"You have sworn on your house," he said, sticking to the script Murphy had given him and Moose had vetted, "but I find I must wonder aloud whether that oath is binding on one so distant from the wellspring of his honor…"

The man's lip curled slightly before he got it under control. "I have no house. I have no other path to a life than that which you and yours offer. I am entirely at your mercy. I live only because your Murphy wills it. The…others we were with would have executed me once they were done interrogating me."

Chalmers noted the care with which the man spoke. Mentioning the SpinDogs by name was a tell he'd been told to watch for.

"And still might do, if you show the least sign of betraying us." Chalmers could play the heavy. Hell, he might even carry through on the threat if his life or Jackson's were threatened.

Yukannak's expression didn't change one iota as he bowed once more.

It made Chalmers nervous, not knowing what the hell the man was thinking. Murphy's file said the guy was *fully* vetted. Murphy's file said Yukannak could probably be relied on for the duration of the mission. Every instinct Chalmers had screamed Yukannak was anything but reliable. But he'd learned from recent misadventures that his instincts could be less than perfect.

Shit, the Mog had taught him that much.

"You have more baggage?" Chalmers asked, putting his misgivings away for the time being.

"Only a few items deemed necessary for the mission." Yukannak gestured at a duffel a few paces deeper in the shadows of the native vegetation.

Chalmers gestured at the additional bag resting at the man's feet. "Drop pod must have been cramped."

A slight smile. "Very. Very cramped."

Chalmers bent to pick up the duffel at their feet, nearly colliding with Yukannak when the man reached for it as well.

A tiny grunt of pain issued from the other man's lips, despite a lack of contact between them.

"You all right?" Chalmers asked.

Yukannak snatched the bag up. "Some bruising from the drop, but nothing to worry about."

Chalmers shrugged and went to get the other duffel. "You can tell me about it on the flight. The sooner we're airborne, the sooner we're out of this hot hell."

* * * * *

Gym Rat Problems

"There you are," Chalmers said, examining the surveillance records tracking the shift sergeant's movement. Every other guy on the downport's security shift had been relatively easy to bribe or blackmail. Not Sergeant Siggun. He was simply not going along with the program, and it had to be third shift. The other shifts were either not in the proper places or would leave the team too exposed to observation from other patrols and checkpoints.

"Options?" he said, stepping back from the notice boards they used to display the various notes and surveillance records for collective review and planning. It was a security risk, but Chalmers wanted input, and this was the best way to get it. They'd lock everything up once they were done, and the staff had already been sent home.

"Liquidate him?" Moose asked, pinning Yukannak's assessment of the survey lighter crew schedule to the board in front of him. He nearly bumped into Jackson as he stood up. The meeting room was crowded between the notice boards, the Lost Soldiers, and Yukannak.

"Jesus," Jackson said, shaking his head. "This ain't the 'Nam, man."

"What, it's an opti—" Moose started.

Chalmers interrupted, "I'd like to do this without smoking too many people. That kind of mayhem will leave a trail we don't want."

"What do we know about him?" Vat asked.

"He doesn't gamble, doesn't visit the happy houses, and isn't in debt to anyone on R'Bak. He does two things aside from eat, sleep, and work: read and hit the gym."

Vat looked thoughtful. "What kind of gym?"

"Not sure," Chalmers said. He glanced at the record again but caught Yukannak's puzzled expression.

"What is it, Yukannak?"

"The question is strange to me."

"What question?"

"There is only one kind of gymnasium on Kulsis."

"Oh?"

"Thega-Tak."

"And what's that when it's at home?" Chalmers asked.

"Their premiere school of unarmed and melee close quarters combat," Vat explained before Yukannak could answer. "From what I've heard at the fights, it's similar to the fighting style we see in the arenas here on the island, but focused on disarming, disabling, and ending resistance as quickly as possible."

"What, you don't lift weights, run, Jazzercize?" Chalmers asked.

"What is 'jazzercize?'" Yukannak asked.

Chalmers shook his head and smiled. "An ancient form of exercise."

"We do other things than this jazzercize in order to build strength and endurance for military operations or Thega-Tak rites."

"Can we pay someone to put him down for a while in the gym, then?" Jackson asked. "Break an arm or something? Engineer some kind of training accident?"

"Hell, get him into the arena and see how he fares?" Chalmers queried, looking at Vat.

"No one from the survey crew fights in the arena," Vat said, looking at Yukannak. "Something about 'pretend fights' being beneath them."

Yukannak nodded. "We do not expose to those beneath us those techniques we may someday be called on to deploy against them. This is especially true of those entrusted with command of those outside their own houses."

"How very...*Übermensch* of your people," Jackson said.

Moose and Chalmers both snorted.

Yukannak must have decided he didn't want to know, because he went on without addressing the comment, "Also, not every survey member is...fully proficient in the techniques, and their participation in such fights might prove an embarrassment to the leadership. I have only recently begun rebuilding my strength, and not every Kulsian has the drive to improve their skill as I do."

Chalmers let that go, thinking that gym rats were the same everywhere and everywhen.

"Do they spar?" Jackson asked. He'd always been more into martial arts than Chalmers.

"Of course."

"So we can set up something where he gets hurt in training?" Jackson insisted.

Yukannak cocked his head. "Perhaps. This man seems very serious in his training regimen, however. That could make it hard to find someone to accomplish your ends."

"Still, it's a better option than attempting to cover up his killing, no?"

A slow nod. "I believe so, given mission parameters. But I think it will be hard to accomplish with local talent. These people are not exactly the best representatives of strong breeding. They are…inferior."

Chalmers saw the quickly-hidden disgust in Jackson's expression as the Lost Soldier asked, "Right, so what do you suggest?"

A small shrug. "I have no suggestions. Only cautions."

"Why not just put something in his drink?" Moose asked.

"They all carry canteens around," Chalmers mused, liking the idea.

"Canteens they do not bring onto the fighting floor," Yukannak added, nodding.

Jackson was smiling. "One problem down?"

Chalmers looked at the others. Seeing no objections, he nodded.

"All right. So let's assume everything else worked, and we've made it onboard. How do we take control without busting up the place?" Jackson said.

"That's the sixty-four-thousand question," Moose said, nodding.

Jackson and Chalmers both looked at Moose, but it was Chalmers who said, "I've heard of the million dollar question, but that's an oddly specific amount."

Moose shrugged. "A game show from when I was a kid."

Chalmers smiled. "I keep forgetting we're all time travelers here."

Yukannak frowned. "I am not. I may not know what a dollar is, but we have to avoid shooting on the bridge or anywhere aboard. Gunfire in any pressurized environment is suicide. You are not trained to fight in microgravity. You will get in each other's way and injure yourselves. And that is assuming you can get to the crew without being detected and then murdered in whatever spot you manage to stow away in. If the crew are the least bit competent and conscious—"

"It's a shit show, we know," Chalmers interrupted, barely keeping his anger in check. He didn't need reminding, the guys didn't need reminding, and he didn't like Yukannak doing the reminding. Not one bit.

"I don't understand your anger. I merely point out facts relevant to your plan of actions."

"Thanks, Captain Obvious," Jackson said.

Chalmers bit his lip to keep from piling on. He really did not like the Kulsian.

"I am not a captain," Yukannak said, gold eyes slitted as he stared back at Jackson.

"No, you're not. You're our pilot," Moose said with a meaningful glance at Chalmers.

Intercede, man! the look begged.

"Moose is right, Yukannak," Chalmers said, careful to keep the reluctance from his voice. "You're our best bet." Chalmers could see Jackson swallowing against gut-level dislike. He continued to speak to Yukannak, looking for the words that would mollify the new man. "And we need your help planning this. Forgive us, as we're very informal in our speech, and find it easy to misunderstand your words just as you find it easy to misunderstand ours. No offense is intended."

Yukannak blinked cold gold eyes. "None taken."

And if I believe that, smack my papa for raisin' a sucker, Chalmers thought, but very carefully, did not say.

*****

Drinking To It

The heat pump kicked on again, even though it was well after sunsdown. It was still well into the hundreds outside the climate-controlled homes and businesses of the island. A grateful Chalmers made another blespa and rum-analogue. He and Vat had been drinking hard for—he squinted at the office clock—a couple of hours, now. Everyone else had gone off to bed as the nightly skull session wound down, but Chalmers had been banging his head against the problem for so long he felt the need to get a little fucked up and forget for a moment how much was riding on their success or failure.

Also, late at night was the only time he felt comfortable enough to really think, now the fast-approaching Sear was making the equator a sunbaked hell. Even the evenings were hot enough to broil the brains, given that the humidity off the water retained a lot of the day's heat when the winds didn't blow.

But the approach of the Sear wasn't his problem. The problems he had were hard enough as it was: how to stow away aboard a lighter, then take that same lighter's crew down in a cramped, pressurized environment—in microgravity, no less—and without giving them a chance to radio for help or breaking important shit like the ship's controls.

"No matter how many firewalls and cut-outs I use to hide my involvement with you guys, I'm still not sure I'll be able to stay here after you've gone," Vat said, drawing Chalmers from yet another go-round with the problems the mission posed.

Glad of the distraction, Chalmers nodded. "I'm sorry about that." He offered Vat his freshly-made drink. "I wasn't clear on why—aside from the money and position—you wanted to stay."

Vat accepted the glass with a wry smile. "I've got a kid."

Chalmers was so surprised he spilled some rum-analogue as he poured a fresh glass for himself. He set the bottle down and picked up the pitcher of iced juice. It held enough ice-cold blespa for maybe one more round.

"But…" he mumbled.

Vat pointed at the floor with one hand. "Here, not back when."

"But…" Chalmers repeated. Vat's answer hadn't exactly clarified matters.

"But I'm gay?" Vat finished.

Chalmers nodded, then drank off a good portion of his glass.

"I am." Vat's smile grew mischievous. "I like men. But desperate times and all that…"

"Desperate ti—" Chalmers snorted.

"Not like that." Vat interrupted. "Not me that was desperate. Just that the local ladies are pretty damn insistent when it comes to making babies with successful fighters…one of 'em, she made it clear I was the donor she wanted." He shook his head. "Not that my reputation ain't a bit overblown." He took a long drink. "Besides, I'm young enough that if you stimulate the equipment in the right way things happen, regardless of where the mind wants to go…"

Chalmers snorted into his drink. He'd enjoyed the advances of a few women since Clarthu, and they'd all been quite clear about what they wanted—and didn't—from him.

"Regardless, the kid exists. And you know the fucked up thing?" Vat's words were quite slurred now.

"No?"

"The fucked up thing is, I want to see him grow up. I want to be there for it. Teach him the shit he needs to know 'bout life."

"Makes s—"

Vat interrupted him again, slurring through another realization, "Christ on a crutch, I want to be a dad, not a daddy."

"Right, man," Chalmers said, uncomfortable. "Jesus, I didn't need to know *that*."

"What, that I'm a daddy, or that I used to want to be a *daddy*?" Vat said. Chalmers saw the man's grin had grown a bit green around the gills.

"Either? Both?"

"Ah, fuck you, Chalmers," Vat said without heat.

Chalmers chuckled, took another drink.

Vat hiccupped, belched wetly, and scratched under his robe. "Hell, why not both daddy *and* dad?"

Chalmers looked at Vat, decided the other man was definitely not getting another drink.

A brief silence fell. Chalmers started thinking about how to take advantage of the firsthand knowledge Yukannak had shared. It might not prove useful, but Chalmers thought it over anyway. None of them had known, for instance, that whatever space was left over in a given lighter crew's supply container, was by tradition, open to freight whatever cargo the crew saw fit to carry. Not on every run, but on missions marked "survey" they were.

He looked through the paperwork, stopping at the shipping schedule they'd bought yesterday. Two weeks of lighter shipping.

One "survey" lighter scheduled for the end of next week. Flight 1517B. The crew consumables container for it would not be ready yet.

"I-I think I might have had too much to drink…"

Hooking it with one leg, Chalmers pushed the trash can across the floor.

Vat turned his head, threw up in the can.

Mostly in the can.

"This is awesome. So. Damn. Awesome," Chalmers said, toasting God, the gods, the Holy Spirit, aliens, humans-who-looked-like-us, whatever. They sure knew how to dick with one Warrant Officer Chalmers.

It wasn't until he was helping the other man into bed that things started clicking into place behind his eyes. One thought led to another to another and then bang!

At first Chalmers sat in the high, narrow hall outside Vat's room, thinking. After an hour or so, he believed he might have figured out how to disable the flight crew. He got up, unsteady at first, and tried the idea out as he paced the halls. He tried to run down all the angles, searching for flaws, playing devil's advocate. Only when he was reasonably sure he had a plan that might work did he wake Jackson and run it by him.

Jackson wiped sleep from his eyes, shook his head. "I'll want you to run all that by me again, once I've had something to wake my ass up."

"Fuck you, I haven't even slept."

Jackson stretched. "And that's my fault, how?"

"It ain't," Chalmers said, tired in his bones. And not just because of the long night. He was tired of the constant tension. Of the not knowing—no, that wasn't accurate; it was the actual *caring* about—who would get hurt. And not just by his actions, but by his failures.

Say one thing about old Chalmers; he'd always felt he had so few options, so little room to maneuver, such limited time between crises, and so much on the line that giving a shit about what his actions might do to other people never really entered into his calculations.

That isn't the case anymore. Not by a long shot.

"I need you to tell me it's ok. That I ain't fucking up. Again."

Jackson was quiet for what seemed like a long time after that.

"I'm fucked, right?" Chalmers said when he couldn't take the suspense any longer.

"Shit, no," Jackson said, holding Chalmers' gaze. "Best I could come up with was to put a bullet in the head of each crewman. In microgravity. With—much as I hate admitting it—a bunch of vital electronics we can't afford the least bit of damage to as the backdrop for our shooting."

Chalmers looked away. "Might still have to, something goes wrong."

"Yeah, but none of us are what you'd call a cold-blooded assassin."

"Right, but still…"

Jackson cocked his head. "It'll be a lot easier on my conscience knowing we tried to avoid killing non-combatants."

"Are they really non-combatants, though?"

Jackson sniffed. "These supremacist fucks still look at everyone else as their inferiors. Sub-humans. Not people. That sort gets what's coming to 'em in my book."

"Couple of ferry pilots hardly constitute the Waffen SS, though."

"No, but all that is required for evil to prevail…"

"Is for good men to do nothing," Chalmers finished.

"And these assholes have been doing a lot more than nothing to ensure the continuance of Kulsis' dominion over R'Bak. So, yeah, push comes to shove, I'll do what's necessary." He looked at Chalmers again. "We all will."

*****

Sweating It

"Papers," the guard said.

"Right here," Chalmers said, handing the folio over. The requested paperwork was sweat-damp, but Chalmers wasn't worried. At least, not about sweaty papers. That was easily explained by the absence of air conditioning for the truck's passenger cab. The short-haul trucks were built on the cheap, and driver comfort was not a concern for the island's overlords, so the cab was still sweltering hot, even in the third hour after sunsdown, and even though the cargo container he was hauling was one of the rare refrigerated models. Couldn't have rations bound for the survey team go bad, now could we?

Even so, he missed his partner's reassuring presence at his side. But Jackson had other work tonight.

The guard took the papers and rifled through them in desultory fashion. The new sergeant remained in the shack beside the gate, his feet up.

Chalmers relaxed fractionally. The bribes they'd been paying were meant to ensure just this kind of *laissez faire* attitude from the guards for Twin Stars trucks, but only when transporting their various cargoes to warehouses, not when moving supplies necessary for a surveyor crew.

"Supplies for flight 1517B?" the guard asked after a moment.

"So I'm told," Chalmers said. He gestured over his shoulder at the cargo container. "Where do I drop it?"

"Hangar Sixteen, last but two on the left."

"Right," Chalmers said. That was good. Sixteen was the proper hangar. They hadn't been sure of that prior to launching this phase of BUCKET. So that part, at least, was according to plan.

The guard motioned at the shack. A moment later the gate dropped.

"Go ahead."

Chalmers put the truck in gear and drove slowly over the gate. He watched in his side mirrors as a hydraulic ram pushed the heavy metal plates upward from below the road surface. Once shoved almost vertical the plates formed an inverted V that was too tall for a man to climb and tough enough to stop any truck on the island cold. Mopping his sweaty brow with the shoulder of his shirt, he picked his canteen up from the seat next to him and took a long pull. Setting the warm can of water down, he pulled his watch from his breast pocket and did the math. Five hours, fifty-five minutes to dawn. Three hours, twenty-three minutes to launch prep.

Jackson would be starting the show any minute now. Chalmers stuffed the watch back in his pocket. Wearing it was out of character. He relied on a mental countdown instead, hoping he wouldn't reach zero.

Chalmers killed the engine as he passed hangar fourteen. The truck rolled to a quiet stop a bit short of Hangar Sixteen's doors. He listened carefully before stepping down from the cab. He pulled a sap from beneath the driver's seat and slipped it into his back pocket. Bypassing the massive hangar doors, he went to the much smaller personnel door near the corner of the building and listened again. Nothing. He tried the door. It opened under his hand.

A man sat at a desk with his back to Chalmers and his feet up. He was breathing deeply, just on the edge of snoring. Chalmers recognized him and stifled a sigh of relief. Supply Officer First Class Justhines was up to his eyeballs in debt, having invested everything he had—including loans from a number of creditors—in purchasing cargo from the various brokerages.

Chalmers grinned and waited. Standing in the open doorway let him enjoy the momentary and slight artificial breeze released from the office as the cold air fled across the threshold to join the heat outside.

The dull thud of the explosion from just outside the wire made Chalmers flinch even though he'd been fully anticipating it. He heaved a relieved sigh. He'd had thirty-five left on his mental countdown.

The supply officer started awake, jumping to his feet.

"What th—"

"A fire! Over at the warehouses," Chalmers said, standing in the doorway and pointing toward the fireball climbing into the sky.

"What?" Justhines said, face contorting as his sleepy mind tried to catch up with what was happening. The supply officer joined Chalmers at the door. His face went white with dread, but he didn't move.

Not wanting to resort to the sap if he didn't have to, Chalmers played it up. "Never thought I'd be so glad to be a simple wage slave. Those that invested too much in cargoes'll lose everything if that fire spreads much more."

That did it. Justhines rushed back into the office and grabbed his duty belt. Buckling it on, he went to the inner door, threw it open, and shouted at the men working in the hangar proper, "You men, grab firefighting gear and meet me out front!"

The pair of cargo technicians working inside leapt to do their officer's bidding.

"What should I do?" Chalmers asked.

"Wait here!"

"But, the shipment..." Chalmers said, hiking a thumb over his shoulder and, in the process, positioning himself to block the door if he had to.

"Right, right," the supply officer yanked the receiver from the cradle and put it to his ear. He started snapping orders into it a moment later.

Chalmers sweated in the doorway. He could see the fire was spreading, but he wasn't really paying attention. Instead, he strained to hear what the officer was saying.

"Looks like it started in the Fangat warehouses," he said into a lull in the phone conversation. "But now it's spreading to the others, too."

"Wha—I don't bloody care what your sergeant says!" The supply officer screamed into the phone. "We have a schedule to keep to, and I'm the duty officer. Get your men into firefighting gear and down to the warehouses, *now!*" He listened for a moment, then snapped, "I'll be there shortly, and I want everyone turned out to fight this fire." Something said to him made the officer look at Chalmers. He turned away. Despite the officer's attempt at quiet, Chalmers still heard him lower his voice and say, "Of *course* no locals. One of *them* might have started the damned fire, you idiot!"

He slammed the phone down.

Chalmers turned and raised a questioning brow. "What do I d—?"

The officer looked him up and down then came to the only decision the plan allowed for. "You'll just have to stay inside the wire for the duration of the emergency."

Chalmers frowned, said grudgingly, "Can I give you and your men a ride?"

"No, someone's coming for us. Get out of my way." He shouldered Chalmers aside and went out the door just as one of their smaller military vehicles, the Kulsian equivalent of a WWII Jeep, rolled up between the truck and the hangar. He looked over his shoulder as he jumped into the open-topped vehicle. Two men hustled out of the main hangar door, leaving it open behind them. They were moving slowly, firefighting gear weighing them down. One of the hangar doors was left ajar as they climbed in behind the driver and their officer.

"I'll bring her in, then?" Chalmers said.

The supply officer nodded. "And get that cargo aboard the lighter!"

"On my own?" Chalmers whined, hoping he wasn't laying it on too thick.

"Yes. That's why we trained you on the lift system! Oh, and get the truck out of there once you're done."

"I'll just sleep in it out here if you aren't back."

"Good. Have it done before I get back, and I'll drop you a few extra coin as well as put in the good word for your brokerage."

"Oh, thank you!" Chalmers called as the vehicle roared away. He couldn't keep a feral grin from his lips as he hurried back to the truck. He paused to strip the tarps bearing the Twin Stars logo from its sides, revealing the Fangat logo. The paperwork inside the truck was Fangat, too. The tarps went into the back of the truck. That done, he climbed into the cab and started the engine. Leaving the truck idling to keep the refrigeration unit running, he went to open the hangar doors the rest of the way.

The lighter was inside, a vast shape that loomed almost two stories tall and stretched all the way into the far end of the hangar. The lighter's flanks were built to accommodate six of the shipping containers on each side, each bay accessible via external hatches and from a central corridor running fore and aft between them. Clamshell hatches closed over the containers in flight, protecting them from re-entry stresses. All but one of them was shut tight, hiding the containers Chalmers had delivered over the last few days. The only open cargo hatch was the one just aft of the crew section. Intended to carry the crew's in-transit consumables, those containers were always loaded last.

"A lot of work for one guy," he huffed as he set his feet and started to push the first door wide.

He walked to the back of the truck and nervously tapped a specific sequence on the metal. A moment's delay, then he heard the answering sequence.

A reassured Chalmers climbed into the cab and drove the truck into the hangar.

Parking beside the massive lighter, Chalmers carefully lined up the container with the lift. Leaving the truck running, he buttoned the hangar up and hurried to the lift controls. He brought the lift bed up and under the container, raising it an inch or so off the truck bed. He took the lift system's remote and hooked it to his belt. Chalmers climbed the external ladder built into the fuselage of the lighter to enter the empty container bay of the interface craft.

Chalmers took the extendable power line from next to the central corridor hatch and returned to the ladder. He dropped the power lines down to the container. Another climb to swap the lines out, shut the truck off, and then had to spend more time he didn't feel he had making sure the load was properly balanced on the lift. He *really* didn't want to have the container slide off while he was loading it. Finalizing the check, Chalmers mopped his brow before climbing the ladder. Again.

So fucking hot, he thought.

Chalmers took a break on reaching the top, wishing he'd been smart enough to remember to clip his canteen to his belt. Parched, he pulled his watch out and put it on. Checked the time. Jackson should be here soon, assuming everything had gone according to plan on his end.

He pulled the remote from his belt and punched the "up" button. Hydraulics whined loudly as they raised the heavy load. Chalmers leaned against the hatch coaming, intending to rest a moment when he realized he'd forgotten the hose. Which was pretty stupid, since without it, the entire mission was hosed. Cursing, he climbed down and retrieved what resembled a narrow-bore fire hose from the back of the truck cab. Looping it over his shoulder, he bent and tapped a knuckle on the passenger side fuel tank. Satisfied it was the one they'd left empty, he attached the hose.

He climbed up again, sweating bullets this time as he unwound the heavy, flattened hose a meter at a time in his wake. On reaching the open hatch, he removed the remaining loops of hose and lay there panting for a short while.

"So fucking thirsty I forgot it again."

He was just standing up when the office door swung open to reveal Jackson.

"You made it," Chalmers called, trying to sound less relieved than he was.

Jackson smiled an immediate reply, but didn't speak. He just stood, bent over with both hands on his knees, and breathed.

Moose entered just as Jackson finally caught his breath. Both men wore dark clothing and face paint that blended easily into the night. Or rather, had worn when they began the operation. Both had sweated so profusely their paint ran from their heads in discolored rivulets.

Recovering first, Jackson closed the office door behind Moose, clapped the bigger man on the back and crossed to the base of the ladder.

"How are my firebugs?" Chalmers asked. The lift continued to rise, cutting Jackson from view unless Chalmers wanted to poke his head out. He did not.

"We're here, ain't we?" Jackson called.

"Fair enough," Chalmers said, biting back an angry retort. What Jackson said was true. If things had gone wrong for either Moose or Jackson, the two were to make for the airport and fly out with Umaren and Vizzel.

The top of the container reached the point he could step out on it. Chalmers stopped the lift. He stood carefully at the container's edge and looked down.

Moose had crossed to join Jackson at the foot of the ladder.

"If you two are finished sucking wind down there, I could use a hand," Chalmers said.

"Right," Jackson said, beginning the climb.

Moose, wiping his brow, looked up and said, "So was this part of your plan? 'Say, let's just take the big guy out and make him run in the heat, then make him climb, then work him like a dog.' Yeh?"

"You slept since what, '69?" Chalmers asked.

"Something like that."

"I'd think you well-rested."

"Fuck you, Chalmers," Moose said, beginning the ascent.

The issue with stowing away on any spacecraft, Yukannak had told them, was that *everything* was repeatedly weighed. The need to effect a weight transfer was why he'd humped a hose up hill and over dale in thousand-degree temperatures. In theory, the weight of every container was checked and then re-checked during pre-flight by flight control planners and then supply officers on the ground. In practice, this procedure was not rigidly adhered to when operational demands necessitated a tight turnaround, let alone when there was some kind of emergency on the ground. The Kulsians were comfortable with this because in the extremely unlikely event of a discrepancy, both mission planners and officers knew sensors in the hold itself would detect any variance from the bill of lading to the actual weight of each cargo container and automatically abort take-off if it was in excess of tolerances.

They'd struggled with how to get around the problem—that any stowaways would trigger those sensors—until Chalmers remembered Umaren's complaints about stripping *Loklis* of A/C parts. It was all about shedding weight in one place so you could add it to another.

Chalmers walked into the central corridor of the lighter and across to bay two, where the last container he'd brought across the wire resided. Checking the manifest to be sure it was the proper one, he smiled. He pushed a specific, palm-sized, section of the container in and to one side. A spigot not unlike a common garden hose bib was mounted within.

He turned to find Jackson stepping off the ladder.

"Hook a brother up?" Jackson said, holding the remaining loops of hose out for Chalmers to connect.

Chalmers grinned and grabbed the hose. He walked into the corridor, hooked it to the master cargo console set beside the hatch to the crew area, and then ran an integral line from the console to the concealed spigot on container two. He made sure the connections were tight and called to Jackson, "We secure down there?"

"Looks good," Jackson said.

"No kinks?"

"Only your own, brother," Moose said.

"Opening." Chalmers tapped the button on the console to begin pumping. A button next to it lit a dull amber. He pressed it home without reading the label.

Liquid gurgled, gushed, and filled the hose as a pump integral to machinery below the console kicked on, pulling liquid from the container to the console and then on down the line and into the truck's empty passenger-side fuel tank. The empty fuel tank would hold the equivalent of seventy-five gallons.

The hose leading through the bay started smoking. Not a real smoke, more like hot Florida pavement struck with a cold rain of the Caribbean.

That's not right, Chalmers thought, sluggish and slow.

Chalmers looked from it to Jackson, who gestured at the console where the hose to the truck connected. Chalmers looked down. The fitting was rimed in smoking ice.

"Did you forget to turn on the heater?" Moose called from outside, a note of alarm in his voice. "'Cause this hose is looking mighty fat."

"Fuck," Chalmers said.

* * * * *

Hot Stuff

Chalmers swallowed against a dry throat and stood to look down on the controls. The button that had glowed amber to warn him of the temperature difference was still lit. He slapped it, but nothing seemed to happen.

He took a second to actually read through all the markings on the console, found one below the button he'd pressed to start the water flow that was marked 'heater.' He jabbed it, hard.

The flow slowed as it was run through a heating coil before being pumped out, but it was already too late. The waxed-fiber hose running from the pump to the truck had been at room temperature, nearly a hundred degrees. The metal fuel tank off the truck, absorbing the heat radiated from the tarmac all day, was even hotter. The water in the cargo container was held at just above freezing. Rapid expansion of the water as it warmed made for a build-up of vapor in the line, leading to gulping back-ups at the truck end of the hose as the air sought a way out of the closed system. Without a release valve, pressure built. With pressure came more heat, which in turn built more air pressure in the line. The hose, made stiff and even somewhat brittle by the cold water rushing through it, was called on to expand to hold the mixture of pressurized air and water. Said pressure mounted until the local-manufactured hose split with a sound like a diarrhea-afflicted giant's extremely wet fart, if said wet fart was sufficiently powerful to tear the farter's pants apart with an accompanying ripping-fabric sound.

"Jesus!" Moose shouted from the hatch. The hangar was gray and misty beyond him as the torn hose continued to vent in great gasping burps.

Chalmers hit the emergency shut-off.

"Shut it down!" Jackson screamed.

"I did!" Chalmers yelled back.

The sound of flowing water and burping hose ends slowly diminished.

Moose, brows drawn together like a thunderhead, turned from looking below and stalked past Jackson toward Chalmers.

Chalmers thought—for just one idiotic instant—about pulling the sap from his pocket to defend himself, but the big man pushed a hand past his shoulder and turned the pump back on.

"Still gotta get all the water out of there."

"Fuck," Chalmers gulped, trembling.

"No use crying over spilt milk," Moose said, not unkindly. "Much as I want to toss you down there for a swim."

Jackson was at the cargo hatch, looking down. He turned to stare at Chalmers. His lips were a thin, bitter line. "Smooth move, ex-lax!"

Chalmers threw his hands up. "How was I supposed to know that would happen?"

"Because Yukannak told us to make sure the water was room temperature before pumping. You either didn't hear him or ignored him because you don't like him. Either way, you done fucked us all."

"Get your panties untwisted, Jackson," Moose rumbled. "That kinda shit ain't helping anyone."

"There's a freaking lake under us and you want me to calm down!?"

Moose sighed and said, "You been through a monsoon before?"

"A what?" Chalmers said at the apparent non sequitur.

"A monsoon, motherfucker," Jackson snapped. Chalmers was hard-pressed to remember when his partner had last been so angry with him.

"More accurately: when the leading edge of a monsoon hits," Moose explained. Seeing nothing but blank stares, he said, "No? Well, the air is dry enough, even on a humid coast, to dry a paved road in a very short time, even at night."

"There a lot of paved roads in Vietnam?" Jackson snarled sarcastically.

"Downtown Saigon? Yeah," Moose said. "Not to mention the airport."

Jackson calmed slightly, still muttering angrily as he climbed down the ladder to secure the tank end of the hose.

"That true?" Chalmers asked quietly.

"Fuck if I know." Moose turned on him, poking a finger into Chalmers' chest as if to emphasize his point. "I *do* know something from personal experience. Back in 'Nam, some guys got it into their heads that fragging leadership was fully justified. It isn't. At least, not during an operation. No matter how much command might deserve a Willie Pete shoved down their throat, during the mission, all is forgiven or all is lost."

Chalmers swallowed, looked away.

"Let's get the rest done, then we can start sweating Lake Chalmers." Moose was grinning as he stepped from the corridor to the container bay.

Failing to see anything funny in the big man's words, Chalmers turned and went to retrieve the necessary tools from the ship's locker.

By the time Chalmers collected the tools and returned to the hold, the mist hanging in the air outside the lighter had cleared and the container had been fully drained of water. Chalmers passed the cargo console. A different amber light glowed a steady warning above the status lights for bay two, the one they were working on. Chalmers grunted in satisfaction. Some things were going to plan. Yukannak had said the light would be red if the weight was too heavy, amber if too light as the latter was far less to worry about than the former.

Moose finished uncovering the last of the concealed bolts securing the end of container two. Chalmers knelt and set the pneumatic wrench to the first bolt. It came free after less than a minute. Nineteen more to go. The work was hot, awkward, and time-consuming, if not terribly difficult. And it was necessary, seeing as each container was inspected by the supply officer after installation and, if not intended to supply the flight crew, affixed with a chemically-treated lead seal to prevent opening. Trying to reattach the seal after penetrating it was simply not something they could do on anything like the operational timeframe they'd have, so Vat had come up with this particular workaround.

"Moose, need you over here," Chalmers said, gesturing with the pneumatic wrench at the front of the container, which was now loose enough to fall forward if unsupported.

Moose dropped the coiled hose off the edge of the container and joined Chalmers.

"Make sure this shit doesn't fall on me." Chalmers blinked sweat from his eyes and blew a raspberry to clear his mouth. "So damn hot," he muttered.

"Got it," Moose said, leaning his bulk against the container front.

Chalmers resumed working. The tenth bolt came free. Eleventh. His world narrowed to the bolt, the wrench, the task. Rinse. Repeat.

"Running out of time, Chalmers," Jackson called from below. Distantly, he heard the cab door slam and the truck start.

"Got it," Chalmers said as the last bolt came free. At least he'd stopped sweating. He stood. The world swayed, steadied. He helped Moose pull the container end free and carefully wrestle the slab of composite material to the deck. The expandable bladder that had contained the frigid water was bunched up by the spigot, leaving a space approximately two meters deep and just under three meters wide on all sides.

"Get the scaffolds set up while I help Jacks?" Chalmers said. He was too tired to trust the accuracy of his work and this next phase was tricky.

Moose took the tools from him and nodded. "Good work, Chalmers."

Chalmers just nodded and staggered out of the bay onto the container-top. The floor of the hangar still shone with damp, but there wasn't a lake to look at. Bone weary, Chalmers sighed and looked at his watch. The mental arithmetic was far harder now than when the night began, but he got there: one hour until flight prep. The fires would be about out by now.

They were on borrowed time.

Jackson had moved the truck outside, was struggling to push the hangar door back into place. He was too close to finishing for Chalmers to get down and be of any real help.

"Can't see the fires anymore," Jackson called. He finished closing the hangar door and jogged across the floor toward the office. He had Chalmers' canteen in his hands. He went into the office, emerged a minute later.

Chalmers did not feel at all well.

"Hey, you take your pills?" Jackson shouted. He was at the base of the ladder. How had Chalmers missed his only friend's approach?

"What?" Chalmers muttered. He staggered, almost fell forward and all the way down, leaned back in alarm, decided to take a seat and fell on his ass atop the container. He blinked, thoughts turgid and slow.

Next thing he knew, Jackson was there.

"Here, drink this." Jackson's voice was worried as he put the canteen to his partner's lips.

"I'm fine."

"No, you're not. You're burning up. Dehydrated as fuck."

Chalmers pulled at the canteen, had to admit the liquid felt phenomenal going down, but then he puked. Dry heaved, really.

"That's not right," he mumbled.

"No, it isn't."

"Keep drinking. Stay put."

"Mmmkay," Chalmers said. He went away for a while.

*****

Sleeping Beauty

Chalmers woke thinking a large woman was sitting on his chest to restrict his air while beating every inch of his flesh. He tried to shake her off, thrashing around, but it did no good. The large woman just clamped one of his wrists in a massive fist.

"Chalmers, cut it out," Jackson said.

Chalmers briefly wondered why his partner was a part of this weird fetish-sex dream he was having, but then realized it was Moose who had him by the wrist and that Jackson was actually yelling at him from his other side.

"What the hell," Chalmers croaked. He had to repeat it, louder. The roar of engines covered anything less than a shout.

"You passed out. Heat stroke," Jackson shouted back.

Chalmers thought about things for a moment. The engine noise was a screaming rumble that made it hard to think. It dawned on him the pressure he'd felt all over and thought was someone trying to suffocate him was actually the G-forces of lift-off.

As if thoughts of the forces at play ended them, Chalmers felt the sudden removal of the weight on his chest. The subsequent full throat and swollen-head feeling of zero-G was even less comfortable. He smiled anyway. They were on their way.

"Holy shit, we pulled it off," Chalmers said, voice reedy and thin to his own ears. His lips were parched, his throat dry where bile wasn't trying to surge up from his belly.

"No shit, Sherlock," Jackson said. His grin was violet in the dim illumination of a R'bakuun chemlight.

"Still not done, snake," Moose said.

Chalmers nodded more soberly. "Jesus, you two had to do everything on your own?"

Jackson shrugged awkwardly against the four-point restraints rigged to the scaffolding. "Nothing new. I'm used to carrying your white ass."

Moose was more serious. "Wasn't that big a deal. I got the scaffolds built and Jackson strapped you in."

They were side by side in the narrow space, half-seated on and half-suspended from the scaffolding that Moose had begun to rig when Chalmers walked out of the hold and passed out. The scaffold was like a seat, but relied on a suspension rig rather than cushions to prevent injury from the rattling associated with high-G maneuvers.

"Everyone else?"

"Still good, last we checked."

"They didn't delay the launch to search for me?"

"Nope. In too much of a rush, just like Yukannak said they'd be."

"How long?"

"Were you out?"

Chalmers nodded.

Jackson checked his watch. "A bit under five hours. You were well and truly cooked, and the A/C unit took a while to chill us out."

"Speaking of which," Moose said. He unhooked a canteen from the scaffold next to him. It had been fitted with a nipple pre-flight to prevent the contents from floating off in microgravity. "Drink up."

Chalmers sucked greedily. There was a weird, almost floral flavor to the water. He swallowed.

"What's in this?"

"It's laced with *hegi* petals tribal healers use to treat dehydration," Moose said.

"Where'd you pick that up?"

Moose slowly spread his hands. "Spent a lot of time around one of the SpinDog docs who trades with the healers at the poles."

"Spent time?" Chalmers said with a half-hearted leer.

"Nothing like that," Moose said flatly. "I don't like to waste time, so I try and pick up new skills as and when I can."

Chalmers wasn't sure what that meant, but the big guy clearly wasn't going to say any more on the subject, so he occupied himself with draining the rest of the canteen. He was already feeling better by the time it was done.

"Bet we smell a treat," Jackson said.

"Speak for yourself, I only smell sweeter the more I sweat," Moose said.

"Bullshit," Chalmers said.

"Just like I've only grown prettier with each passing year," Moose continued.

"And your wedding tackle's bigger?" Jackson grinned.

"Nah, can't improve on perfection," Moose said, lacing his fingers behind his head, the motion somewhat ruined when one of his elbows caught on the container wall.

The partners stifled laughter. It was unlikely they'd be heard through the container wall, the bulkhead, hatch, and several meters of corridor to the cockpit, but shit could happen and probably would, given their luck. Murphy's Law, after all.

Chalmers looked to his left and right, and decided—shit luck or no—he'd rather not have anyone else along on this particular ride with him. They just had to survive the next thirty-plus hours of claustrophobic inactivity, take over a spaceship without getting killed or breaking anything important, and then join up with a group of recently-unreliable allies.

"Easy-peasey," Chalmers mumbled. He waited a beat, then added, "Not that I need to, yet, but where do we piss?"

* * * * *

Playing Scotty

A faint vibration woke Chalmers from a half-doze. It was repeated a little while later. He stretched to ease a cramp and bumped against Moose's shoulder. He checked his watch: twenty-five hours in. He looked up from it to see Jackson was watching him. His partner flicked his gaze to the container wall and pressed a finger to his lips.

"I think…" Moose's whisper was hoarse.

Chalmers looked at him, but the big veteran had his eyes closed. "What?" he said after a moment.

Moose gestured him to silence with one hand. The other was flat against the container wall in front of them.

Chalmers looked at his watch and waited a full minute without hearing anything before whispering, "What is it?"

"Shh…" Moose laid his other hand on the wall.

Chalmers did the same, just in time to feel a faint vibration through the composite. He looked over at Moose to find the other man's eyes open, and his mouth set in a thin line.

"What was that?"

Moose looked at him and whispered, "I think…a container door is open. It keeps hitting the bulkhead every ten seconds or so."

"Did one of you hear the corridor hatch open? Someone walking out there?"

"No," both men said.

"Who would leave a container doo—" Jackson started.

Chalmers popped a cold sweat. "Fucking *Yukannak*."

"Jesus," Jackson swore.

Moose put his hands to the latch for the container doors and looked a question at Chalmers.

Chalmers hit the release on his harness. Jackson did the same beside him. They both braced themselves. Prepared to launch himself out, Chalmers nodded at Moose. He unlatched and threw open the doors, which clanged against the bulkhead and sent the torn inspection seal flying free to join the one from Yukannak and Vat's container. Jackson and Chalmers were both out and almost inside container one before the doors started to rebound.

Vat hung in his harness, unconscious or dead. Yukannak was conspicuous in his absence.

Chalmers launched himself for the cargo console and paged through some data until he found the graphic for the crew's remaining drinking water. Not quite halfway to the point they'd figured sufficient to knock them out.

"I'll take care of Vat if he's still kicking," Jackson said.

Moose bounced from the corridor wall to grab a convenient rung next to the console. He pointed with his chin at the touch panel next to the hatch.

Chalmers looked. Bypass clips were hooked into wires within the panel. The floating face of the panel still glowed a steady green, indicating the portal remained unlocked.

"Why go before they were fully dosed?" Moose asked.

Chalmers shrugged, resultant inertia nearly pulling him from the console.

Jackson didn't turn from Vat. "Because he wanted time to talk them into backing his play, and them being a little loose from the drugs would only make it easier..."

Chalmers launched himself across at the hatch leading to the regular crew module. "And just because the *plan* called for them to consume more, didn't mean it was strictly necessary. We were erring on the side of caution. Wanted them good and soused when we came out."

"Shit."

"Yeah."

"So, what do we do now?" Moose's knuckles were white where he clutched at the rung.

Chalmers swallowed. "Go after him—them. Fast and hard."

"Right." Moose pushed off, fetched up against the hatch leading to the crew spaces.

Vat moaned. Jackson turned from him. "He's unconscious, but he'll be fine. Looks like Yukannak slipped him the same mickey we were giving the crew, only he got the full dose."

Relief flooded Chalmers. As much because he wanted Jacks next to him in a fight as for the news of Vat's condition. He pushed off for the side opposite Moose and caught himself with a minimum of flailing. Moose already had his sap thonged to his wrist. Chalmers pulled his out and did the same with it.

"We need to move fast once we open this," Moose said.

"Tell me again why they won't just vent the atmosphere when we appear?" Chalmers asked.

"According to the SpinDogs, venting atmosphere is a good way to get launched off course very rapidly, not to mention a waste of resources," Moose said.

"But even if the Kulsis assholes think the same way guys brought up in orbital habs do, they might try it outta spite," Jackson said, joining them at the hatch. "And in that case, we should have a bunch of visible warnings as they override the safety measures to vent atmosphere." He held up his sap. "At which point it's crackin' crackers' faceplates 'till they think better of the idea."

Listening to Jackson, Chalmers felt a surge of confidence that simply wouldn't withstand rational analysis. Deciding not to overthink it, he rode it.

Moose looked at them both. His sweat-streaked paint job made him look vaguely clownish—or rather, like a militaristic version of the clown-creature in *It*. "Much as I like watching you two wind each other up, the more time we spend here, the more time Yuk has to pull shit. We need to go."

The crew module had crew cabins aft of the hatch to the cargo bays, a small mess/briefing room immediately beneath it, and the bridge—flight deck, really—forward of it. Each had its own hatch. "So," Chalmers said aloud. "Down this hatch, forward to the bridge hatch, through it, and take out whoever is at the controls. Regroup, head aft and deal with anyone behind. Jacks in the lead, me next, Moose bringin' up the rear."

"Right," Jackson and Moose chorused.

"Go."

Moose pressed the panel. The hatch irised open.

Jackson pulled himself through first, launching headfirst between the decks. Chalmers came second, turning to watch the crew cabins. The short corridor that let out on the cabins was empty and silent, their individual hatches closed.

Seeing no one, Chalmers tried to look the other way. He only succeeded in imparting a spin to his movements. 'Below' him, Jackson bounced on his hands and shoved off toward the bridge. Chalmers was less graceful about it, banging his shoulder painfully as he rebounded off the deck.

Moose managed to not only grab Chalmers but hook both feet under a pair of grab bars. Grunting with effort, he hauled back and launched Chalmers toward the hatch.

Stifling the urge to puke as his ears and eyes disagreed with which way he was traveling, Chalmers prepared to stick his landing this time.

He coasted past Jackson, who was pulling himself forward hand over hand.

This hatch wasn't rigged like the one between crew module and cargo bays, leading Chalmers to wonder just where the hell Yukannak was.

Chalmers brushed a couple grip bars, slowing his rush to the hatch.

"Try it and see," Jackson said quietly.

Chalmers realized that if the hatch opened under his touch, Jacks was lined up to fly straight through without slowing. Thinking he probably looked like a shitty Superman, he reached out and punched the panel.

The hatch irised open. Jacks went through.

Neither of the crew were suited. The pilot looked over, a dopey grin on his face. That grin barely had opportunity to congeal before Jackson was on him. Moose flew through, blocking Jackson and the pilot from view.

Chalmers pulled himself into the crowded flight deck just as Moose swung his sap at the man punching buttons at the engineering station. The engineer shoved back from his work station. Moose missed, momentum from his swing carrying him around in an unsteady—and uncontrolled—spin.

Chalmers launched himself at the engineer, who was struggling free of his seat webbing. He heard a meaty thump and hoped it was Jackson cracking the pilot a good one rather than Moose knocking himself out on a bulkhead. Then there was no time for thought. He grabbed the frame of the engineer's chair in his off hand, punched out with the sap in hopes of losing less body control on a miss, and clipped the engineer's shoulder instead of his chin. The man grunted, popped the rest of the way out of the restraint system, and somehow managed a strike to Chalmers' gut.

Wind whistling as it fled his lungs, Chalmers swung around the pivot-point of his death grip on the chair, wrenching his wrist with the sudden, awkward change of direction.

The engineer kicked out at Chalmers, or tried to. The odd booties Kulsis spacers wore struck a control. Something glowed an angry red in response.

Releasing the weapon to swing from his wrist, Chalmers shoved hard off the deck with his sap hand and legs. He spun back around, his pivot-wrist shrieking protest. His fist missed. The sap, on its several inches of thong, did not. Something gave way with an audible crack, but Chalmers was too busy slamming his chest against the chair to know what. Wheezing, he tried to keep station and see what was happening, what needed doing next.

The engineer was floating gently back toward the hatch, motionless.

A bloody-faced Jackson was straddling the pilot's chair while hammering his sap at the occupant. There was a lot of blood in the air around them, and the pilot didn't look like he was fighting back.

"Jackson," Moose called. "Ease up. We'll need him." The big soldier drifted slowly forward.

Jackson looked their way.

Chalmers swallowed. The hate in Jackson's eyes was limitless. His partner's face was a bleak ruin, his right eye swollen completely shut and his jaw visibly misaligned. Bloody bubbles expanded from his nostrils with each tortured breath, expanded, grew to impossible size and popped.

"Easy, brother. Easy," Chalmers said.

Jacks mumbled something, madness fading from his eyes. He unlocked from his three-point grip on both pilot and his chair. He and the body beneath him drifted apart. If there was any question, the shit stink proved the pilot was dead.

"Hit 'm so 'rd," Jackson mumbled. "Thut I wuh dead. 'Urts."

Chalmers reached out, took Jackson gently by the arm, and eased him into the engineering seat.

An alarm klaxon sounded. Chalmers looked down. The angry red light he'd seen in the engineering console was flashing now. "What the fuck?" he said, struggling to decipher the unfamiliar data.

Moose had grabbed the engineer.

"He all right?" Chalmers asked, half-hoping the guy could be convinced to help.

"Dead," Moose said, towing the engineer toward the hatch.

"What?" Chalmers blurted.

"Temple's bashed in."

"Fuck."

"Can you shut that alarm off?" Moose asked. He opened the hatch and shoved the body out.

"I'm not even sure I know what system it is," Chalmers snapped. "Looks like a countdown of some sort."

"Countdown to what?"

"Do I look like fucking Scotty to you?"

"I'm not looking at you. I'm watching our six, like a good rear guard is supposed to. Yukannak is still outstanding. Jackson is down for the count."

Suddenly fearful, Chalmers glanced at his partner. Jackson was out cold but breathing. Even minor injuries incurred in microgravity could be a very real problem. Simple swelling could get out of control with no pull to direct the fluid in a given direction.

"Focus, Chalmers. One problem at a time," Moose said. "Get a read on what the hell is going on with engineering."

Getting a grip on his incipient panic, Chalmers started to sort through the various read-outs he could access. A lot of it was locked down behind a security wall. He was sweating and his wrist throbbed, distracting him. Near as he could tell, the engineer had been busy with something to do with the power plant. He'd...Chalmers checked the readings, panic mounting.

"Fuck," Chalmers breathed. He scanned through another set of reports. The engineer had intentionally removed a section of shielding on the power plant. He tried to undo it, but ran into a request for a password or fingerprints. He ran at it another way, figured out that whatever the engineer had done, they'd also remote-locked the engineering console located in engineering.

"What?" Moose said. His usual calm voice was ground thin with impatience.

"Not sure, give me a minute," Chalmers said, checking additional radiation meters further up the vessel. He breathed a sigh of relief. The power plant was well enough back in the ship the radiation leak wouldn't reach them with anything like a lethal dose. Not in the next few hours, anyway.

"Get me the engineer."

"I told you, he di-di mau'd, dead as dirt."

"He's still got fucking hands, don't he?" Chalmers snapped.

* * * * *

Engineering Space

The lights flickered, went out, came back on red.

"Chalmers, what the hell is going on?" Moose asked, coasting back onto the flight deck, engineer in tow.

"Automated visual warning system in case of loss of atmosphere," Chalmers read, taking the dead man by the arm.

"Warning for what?"

"Radiation levels are increasing beyond engineering…" Chalmers slapped the corpse's left hand down on the console.

Nothing happened.

"What?" Moose's voice was strained to the point of breaking. A glance showed the big guy pale beneath his paint. It figured that anyone who grew up in the late forties or early fifties could fully ignore the existential threat of nuclear radiation. Praying it would work, Chalmers grabbed the corpse's right hand and flattened it against the console.

SYSTEM UNLOCKED glowed in big red letters.

"Look man," Chalmers said, trying to play it cool as he accessed the previously-secured systems beyond the print lock. "I'm no fucking engineer, but something weird was goi—," Chalmers stopped speaking when one edge of the panel started pulsing. He read it aloud. "Engineering comm."

"What?"

Chalmers ignored Moose, tapped the corner.

A speaker came to life. "Replace the shielding, and I'll surrender."

Chalmers recognized Yukannak's voice with some difficulty. The engineering section had an ear-piercing radiation warning sounding at loud intervals.

"Wh—" Moose began. He stopped when Chalmers raised a hand.

Chalmers faked a baritone and summoned his best Kulsis accent. "Why should we not let you cook until your testicles will no longer serve to sire another generation?"

"Because I can deliver the rest of the stowaways."

Chalmers thought quickly, waved Moose out the hatch. "We have them already."

Moose looked at him for an instant, then nodded. He launched himself out the door.

"Do you have them all, though?"

Chalmers called up the hatch control graphic. "The only one outstanding is you, and I have you where I want you," Chalmers said, voice echoing as it was rebroadcast on every comm throughout the ship.

"I could do a great deal of damage here." Something in Yukannak's tone set Chalmers' teeth on edge. He watched the graphic, tracking Moose's progress through the ship.

"And die in the process?" he said, trying to visualize the position of the engine-room console in relation to the hatch. He was fairly certain the seat locked in a rear-facing position when it was unmanned, and required the occupant to unlock it when taking the position.

"I understand I wronged you by starting this the way I did," Yukannak said, even tones belying what had to be a stressful situation. "But I had limited options, and I believed you would be compromised by the drugs those who brought me aboard introduced into your supplies."

Between beats of the alarm, Chalmers remembered the dopey expression the pilot had worn on entry to the flight deck and decided he'd been only too ready with his own responses and too quick with his answers. He added a slight slur to his words. "Anger accomplishes many things."

"A wonder of evolution," Yukannak agreed.

A 'lock override request' came up for the hatch leading to engineering. Chalmers' hand hovered over the accept graphic, praying Moose could get in fast and overwhelm the traitor. He paused, resolved to do what he could to distract Yukannak.

"Tell me again why you—"

"Betrayed the creatures with me?" Yukannak interrupted.

"Yes," Chalmers said.

"Once you let me out of here."

"How do I know you won't resist further?"

"Because I have lost all advantage. It would be foolish to continue. You have proven my superior."

Chalmers hesitated, thinking through the angles. "You will strap yourself into the console and remain there while we decide what to do with you."

In the relative silence between ringing of the klaxon Chalmers half-heard a noise like an indrawn breath, but no words.

The channel went dead.

Shit. I should never have said 'we.' Kulsians do not reach a consensus before acting.

Another comm request light blinked, this one from the cargo bay corridor.

Making sure it was private, Chalmers tapped it open and said, "I fucked up, Moose."

"I heard. Do I go?"

"I'd join you, but there's no time-delay on the door control."

"Copy. I think I can take him."

"You sure?"

"We got much choice?"

"Could just let him cook."

"And let him figure out a way to do us more harm from in there?"

"Right. Tell me when."

Chalmers swallowed. "Wait one." He muted Moose, piped the channel throughout the ship, and dialed up engineering.

A pause, then, "Chalmers?"

"Sure is," he said, dropping into his normal voice.

"I didn't kill any of you, even when I could have."

"I know." And then, because he had only one card left to play, Chalmers said, "It's the only reason you're slow roasting instead of dead already."

"How did you get control of the bridge?" Yukannak said.

"We followed the plan," Chalmers said, loading his voice with contempt. "You know, the one that would have seen us all safely in command."

"But the lockouts…Di—"

"You can't have believed we would reveal all our capabilities to you, a traitor to your own people?"

An indrawn breath, then, "What do you want of me?"

"Surrender. Immediate and unconditional."

Chalmers heard a sound he recognized: hands slapping a console like the one in front of him. Two hands. The console was not far from the door.

"What kind o—" Yukannak started.

"That is my only, final offer!" Chalmers shouted over him, hoping the sound of his voice would cover the sound of the hatch unlocking.

"What are—?"

Chalmers heard a grunt, followed quickly by a heavy impact. A moan, then a spluttering wheeze.

"Fucker!" Moose yelled, grunting with exertion. More struggles. More gasps.

"Want me down there?" Chalmers half-shouted.

"No, he's gonna go night-night soon," Moose said, hoarse with effort.

"What?"

"Isn't that right, Yuks?" Moose hissed. "Say goodnight."

A gurgle. A gasp. More gurgles.

"Choked him out, Chalmers. Come get him. I ain't letting go of this asshole 'til you got him hogtied."

"On my way."

*****

A Reckoning

"There's a big difference between swearing innocence and admitting a degree of culpability. I did attempt to take the ship alone, thinking I had a better chance of success that way. In the end, my actions assisted you in the taking of this vessel. Were it not for my actions distracting the crew, you'd not have taken them down so easily."

"Easily?" Chalmers snarled. "Look at Jackson, you smug fuck!"

Yukannak's golden gaze didn't even flick Jackson's way. He shrugged as much as his bindings would allow. Which was not a great deal. He was hogtied, and suspended a good meter away from anything he could possibly reach. The muscle the Kulsian had built up while training with them was a threat they would not be underestimating again anytime soon.

"I warned you all that sons of Kulsis are not easily overcome in hand-to-hand fighting. Especially those who lay claim to a command." Yukannak cocked his head at Jackson, eyes never leaving Chalmers. "There lies proof of the truth of my words."

"Didn't stop Moose from kicking your ass, did it?" Chalmers said. Despite the brave words, he couldn't help looking at his partner's still form.

Jackson's head was a mass of bandages meant to keep his jaw in one place. They'd sedated him with some of the drugs meant for the crew, and he was breathing normally now, but none of them were real medics, let alone doctors.

"I believed your plan insufficient to the task," Yukannak said. "I told you this before we embarked on the mission. You did not listen.

I only took action in order to prevent my own demise. Any miscalculation on my part worked to your benefit, landing you in command of the vessel."

Chalmers looked at the Kulsian. Yukannak didn't look that much better. His right ear was missing a big chunk where a blow from Moose's sap had torn it, his left cheek was swollen around a visible break in the underlying bone, and his lips were split in several places.

"What were you going to do if you managed to take the ship?"

"Use knowledge of your presence to assure my own survival, of course. Disrupting ongoing survey operations is an offense which carries a death sentence under normal circumstances."

"And these are anything but?"

Yukannak smiled, causing spherical beads of blood to form on his split lips. "You understand more than you let on, Chalmers."

Moose coasted into the room sailing right past Yukannak. Chalmers took a bully's pleasure in watching the Kulsian flinch away from Moose as the big Lost Soldier hooked a bruise-mottled arm through a convenient rung to arrest his flight. He looked from Chalmers to Yukannak and said, "Vat says he's got a good read on our rendezvous."

"I hope, for all our sakes, that no emergencies arise." Yukannak's blood-dotted grin reappeared. "Emergencies such as those that require a skilled pilot at the controls of this ship."

Moose reached out and casually slapped the back of the Kulsian's head with one big mitt. "Can't exactly trust you at the controls, can we? Just like fuckin' ARVN. Never knew when they'd been bought out by the dope peddlers or the fuckin' VC."

Yukannak glared at his captors. "I only did what I knew to be the best option for my survival. My actions would have also ensured your survival as well."

"Sure, as POWs," Moose said.

"Hell, we *untermensch* would have been accorded even less rights than any POWs the Viet Cong kept. I bet we'd have all been eager to play Russian roulette a la that scene in *The Deer Hunter* after a day or two as their prisoner."

"Chris Walken was *amazing* in that flick," Vat said, pulling himself into the galley from the flight deck.

Moose looked puzzled.

"Another great movie, brother," Chalmers explained.

"That we'll never see again," Vat added sadly.

"You are all nostalgic for so many things that mean nothing," Yukannak said, contemptuous. "And all while you should be focused on survival. It will be your undoing."

"Should have let you cook," Chalmers snapped.

Moose grinned. "I'm already nostalgic for a scene like that."

"No good if I can't watch that smug expression die," Vat opined.

Jackson mumbled something. They'd set his dislocated jaw while he was unconscious, but the hinges or whatever had swollen so big as to make him look like a chipmunk.

Chalmers drifted over toward him. "Don't speak, man. Go back to sleep."

His partner's one visible eye was open. It slowly focused on Chalmers.

"Hard to," Jackson mumbled, slowly and carefully, "with you bastards arguing."

"Hey, I seem to remember waking up all swathed in bandages—mostly *unnecessary* bandages—while you performed a little drama for my entertainment," Chalmers said, a strained feeling building in his chest. "I'm afraid arguing with the fucker who was gonna sell us out was the best I could do on short notice."

A slight stirring beneath the bandages, a sighed shadow of a chuckle that cut to a pained cough.

"Sorry, man," Chalmers whispered.

Jackson didn't reply, eye drifting closed on another wave of dope.

Chalmers felt a selfish need to keep Jackson awake: to ask him for, and receive, his approval. His absolution for everything that had gone wrong since they'd boarded the Blackhawk in Mogadishu.

Sitting on the feeling, Chalmers analyzed the need for reassurance, realized he wanted to know that he hadn't fucked everything up. That doing his best had, just this once, been *enough*.

Vat appeared at his elbow. "He's a tough bastard, Chalmers. He'll be all right."

"We're all tough bastards, ain't we?" Chalmers said. "But I'm the one who let us get blindsided."

"What?" Moose said.

Chalmers swallowed past a lump in his throat. "My decisions," he said hoarsely, "led to this. I didn't...I should have...seen that fucker coming." He fixed Yukannak with a stare. All the hate he felt—toward his situation, toward his old life, toward himself—he channeled into that withering glare.

Yukannak didn't look away, but his grin froze then broke under the stare.

Chalmers kept staring until Moose drifted between them. "I'll just move this garbage to a cabin for the time being." He untethered Yukannak from the bulkhead and towed him out of the mess.

Chalmers forced his fists to unclench as the men disappeared into the cabin. His wrist throbbed in time with his too-fast pulse.

Vat cleared his throat. "You know, I didn't think we'd pull it off."

Chalmers chuckled, said sourly, "Have we?"

"Have we what?"

"Have we pulled it off?"

"I have to believe we have," Vat said. He nodded, once and sharply, as if convincing himself. "Bowden and crew will rendezvous with us in a couple days. We get off, report, go home. Everyone is happy."

"Home?" Another, more forceful, laugh escaped Chalmers' lips. It was no less sour than the chuckle, though.

Vat shrugged. "Well, for certain values of home, anyway."

"Right. That's the thing, ain't it?"

"What?"

"We ain't ever going back. Not going home. Not in any real sense."

"You just now figuring that out?"

Chalmers looked down at his hands. "I suppose so. It's just…"

"Just what?"

"Just…" Chalmers sighed, raised his hands as he tried to explain what bothered him. "I was happy to be here at first. Had all these plans to make myself a better…person. I didn't really think that all the way through, though."

"How's that? Sounds kinda admirable to me."

Chalmers glanced at Jackson. Eyes skipping from the bandaged body back to Vat's questioning face, he shrugged. "I just realized I don't know that making me better is worth two shits if there's no one to go home to, to be better *for*, you know?"

Vat smiled crookedly. "I only know what works for me. Family—chosen or born into—is the only thing worth fighting for."

"Even when all you're fighting against is your own inclination to do wrong?"

"Especially then."

He cast another look at Jackson. "I suppose it does," Horace Earl Chalmers said with a somber nod. "I suppose it does."

#####

About Griffin Barber

Griffin spent his youth in four different countries, learning three languages, and burning all his bridges. Finally settled in Northern California with a day job as a police officer in a major metropolitan department, he lives the good life with his lovely wife, crazy-smart daughter, and needy dog. *1636: Mission to the Mughals*, co-authored with Eric Flint, was his first novel. *1637: The Peacock Throne* came out in May of 2021. He's collaborated with Kacey Ezell on a novel set in their Last Stop Station Universe, titled *Second Chance Angel.* He's also collaborated with Chuck Gannon, penning *Man-Eater*, the third in the six-part first season of Murphy's Lawless.

He has a number of short stories set in different universes coming out in 2022.

* * * * *

Find out what's coming from CKP!

Join the Factory Floor and stay in touch!

Meet us at: https://www.facebook.com/groups/461794864654198/

* * * * *

The Caine Riordan Universe

The Caine Riordan series and Terran Republic universe deliver gritty yet doggedly optimistic hard scifi in a world that is a believable and embattled successor to our own. For those who are not familiar with the series' hallmark blend of exploration, alien encounters, intrigue, and action, you can find them all right here:

The **Caine Riordan** series
(Baen Books)
Fire with Fire
Trial by Fire
Raising Caine
Caine's Mutiny
Marque of Caine
Endangered Species (forthcoming)

The **Murphy's Lawless** series
(Beyond Terra Press)
Shakes
Obligations
Man-Eater
Promises
Pearl
Waveoff
Murphy's Lawless

The **Murphy's Lawless: Watch the Skies** series
(Beyond Terra Press)
Sundown
Firefall
Shadows
Murphy's Lawless: Watch the Skies

The **Murphy's Lawless: Mission Critical** series
(Beyond Terra Press)
Infiltration
Insertion (forthcoming)
Assault (forthcoming)
Murphy's Lawless: Mission Critical (forthcoming)

Other works in the **Terran Republic** universe
(Beyond Terra Press)
Lost Signals

Since that list includes a winner of the Compton Crook Award, four Nebula finalists, and ten Dragon Award finalists, they're not hard to find. Just go wherever books are sold. Want to learn more about the Caine Riordan series? Easy. Contact any of the publishers, or you can reach out to me at contact@charlesegannon.com.

Want to see more of what's going on in the Terran Republic universe? Check out http://www.charlesegannon.com for exclusive written and visual content.

And if you decide you don't want to miss a single new release or announcement, then go to http://charlesegannon.com/wp/sign-up/ to join the all-inclusive mailing list for sneak peeks, special offers, and features you won't see anywhere else.

And most important of all…welcome aboard; we're glad you're here!

The following is an

Excerpt from Book One of the Revelations Cycle:

Cartwright's Cavaliers

Mark Wandrey

Available Now from Seventh Seal Press

eBook, Paperback, and Audio Book

Excerpt from "Cartwright's Cavaliers:"

The last two operational tanks were trapped on their chosen path. Faced with destroyed vehicles front and back, they cut sideways to the edge of the dry river bed they'd been moving along and found several large boulders to maneuver around that allowed them to present a hull-down defensive position. Their troopers rallied on that position. It was starting to look like they'd dig in when Phoenix 1 screamed over and strafed them with dual streams of railgun rounds. A split second later, Phoenix 2 followed on a parallel path. Jim was just cheering the air attack when he saw it. The sixth damned tank, and it was a heavy.

"I got that last tank," Jim said over the command net.

"Observe and stand by," Murdock said.

"We'll have these in hand shortly," Buddha agreed, his transmission interspersed with the thudding of his CASPer firing its magnet accelerator. "We can be there in a few minutes."

Jim examined his battlespace. The tank was massive. It had to be one of the fusion-powered beasts he'd read about. Which meant shields and energy weapons. It was heading down the same gap the APC had taken, so it was heading toward Second Squad, and fast.

"Shit," he said.

"Jim," Hargrave said, "we're in position. What are you doing?"

"Leading," Jim said as he jumped out from the rock wall.

* * * * *

Find out more about Mark Wandrey and the Four Horsemen Universe at:

https://chriskennedypublishing.com/the-four-horsemen-books/

* * * * *

The following is an

Excerpt from Book One of the Salvage Title Trilogy:

Salvage Title

Kevin Steverson

Available Now from Theogony Books

eBook, Paperback, and Audio Book

Excerpt from "Salvage Title:"

The first thing Clip did was get power to the door and the access panel. Two of his power cells did the trick once he had them wired to the container. He then pulled out his slate and connected it. It lit up, and his fingers flew across it. It took him a few minutes to establish a link, then he programmed it to search for the combination to the access panel.

"Is it from a human ship?" Harmon asked, curious.

"I don't think so, but it doesn't matter; ones and zeros are still ones and zeros when it comes to computers. It's universal. I mean, there are some things you have to know to get other races' computers to run right, but it's not that hard," Clip said.

Harmon shook his head. *Riiigghht,* he thought. He knew better. Clip's intelligence test results were completely off the charts. Clip opted to go to work at Rinto's right after secondary school because there was nothing for him to learn at the colleges and universities on either Tretra or Joth. He could have received academic scholarships for advanced degrees on a number of nearby systems. He could have even gone all the way to Earth and attended the University of Georgia if he wanted. The problem was getting there. The schools would have provided free tuition if he could just have paid to get there.

Secondary school had been rough on Clip. He was a small guy that made excellent grades without trying. It would have been worse if Harmon hadn't let everyone know that Clip was his brother. They lived in the same foster center, so it was mostly true. The first day of school, Harmon had laid down the law—if you messed with Clip, you messed up.

At the age of fourteen, he beat three seniors senseless for attempting to put Clip in a trash container. One of them was a Yalteen, a member of a race of large humanoids from two systems over. It wasn't a fair fight—they should have brought more people with them. Harmon hated bullies.

After the suspension ended, the school's Warball coach came to see him. He started that season as a freshman and worked on using it to earn a scholarship to the academy. By the time he graduated, he was six feet two inches with two hundred and twenty pounds of muscle. He got the scholarship and a shot at going into space. It was the longest time he'd ever spent away from his foster brother, but he couldn't turn it down.

Clip stayed on Joth and went to work for Rinto. He figured it was a job that would get him access to all kinds of technical stuff, servos, motors, and maybe even some alien computers. The first week he was there, he tweaked the equipment and increased the plant's recycled steel production by 12 percent. Rinto was eternally grateful, as it put him solidly into the profit column instead of toeing the line between profit and loss. When Harmon came back to the planet after the academy, Rinto hired him on the spot on Clip's recommendation. After he saw Harmon operate the grappler and got to know him, he was glad he did.

A steady beeping brought Harmon back to the present. Clip's program had succeeded in unlocking the container. "Right on!" Clip exclaimed. He was always using expressions hundreds or more years out of style. "Let's see what we have; I hope this one isn't empty, too." Last month they'd come across a smaller vault, but it had been empty.

Harmon stepped up and wedged his hands into the small opening the door had made when it disengaged the locks. There wasn't enough power in the small cells Clip used to open it any further. He put his weight into it, and the door opened enough for them to get inside. Before they went in, Harmon placed a piece of pipe in the doorway so it couldn't close and lock on them, baking them alive before anyone realized they were missing.

Daylight shone in through the doorway, and they both froze in place; the weapons vault was full.

* * * * *

Get "Salvage Title" now at:
https://www.amazon.com/dp/B07H8Q3HBV.

Find out more about Kevin Steverson and "Salvage Title" at:
http://chriskennedypublishing.com/.

*****

Made in United States
Troutdale, OR
09/17/2023

12987425R00086